THE OTHER GARDEN

THE OTHER GARDEN

Francis Wyndham

Moyer Bell Limited
Mt. Kisco, New York

LIBRARY OF CONGRESS
CATALOGING IN PUBLICATION DATA

Wyndham, Francis
The Other Garden
London : J. Cape.
I. Title.

PR6073.Y67084 1988 823'.914 88-1549

ISBN 0-918825-78-4

For David and Judy

Faut-il partir? rester? Si tu peux rester, reste;
Pars, s'il le faut.

Charles Baudelaire,
'Le Voyage'

I

'How soon will lunch be ready?' my father would ask. Assuming that hunger had made him impatient, my mother would answer with eager apology, 'Oh, any minute now – it must be nearly one.' But she had misinterpreted him. He had really wanted to know if he still had time for a further look at the other garden before sitting down to the meal. In dismay, she would watch him put on an old grey trilby hat, choose a stick, pass purposefully through the front entrance, then walk serenely down the short drive and vanish into the open road. Almost immediately opposite, a painted white wooden door in a red brick wall admitted him to this beloved extension of his property, subtly but certainly separate from the house and its bland surrounding lawns. Once in the other garden he was safely out of earshot – but a few minutes later I would be sent in search of him with a summons to return, the serving of our food having been innocently hastened by his ambiguous question when what he had hoped for was delay.

He had designed the other garden himself. It was in the formal tradition, of an artificially geometric kind already unfashionable in the mid-1930s and later to become more so: an almost perfect square enclosing yews clipped into animal shapes, low box hedges, crescent and oval flower beds, circles and triangles of mown grass embellished by stone bird-baths and straight symmetrical paths converging on a central sundial. Four ornamental benches stood at the corners of the intricate pattern thus composed; the

9

vegetable garden and tool-sheds were screened from this purely decorative expanse by tall rows of sweet peas and raspberry canes. The whole lay on a slope above the main street of the village, so that facing south one could look past the roofs of the houses down to the river beyond, and across the damp green water-meadows in the valley up to the steeper hill on the other side. This commanding position gave a slightly vertiginous feeling, as if the ground had suddenly tilted to topple one, and also an exciting consciousness of being unusually exposed: people, after all, might be looking back from the village at the denizens of the garden.

The view to the north was reassuring: there, unexpectedly close, were the stable buildings and thick trees only partly hiding the place where we lived just over the invisible road. To be in the other garden, therefore, could to the senses of a small child combine the exotic with the familiar, the adventurous with the secure. As in the half-remembered excursions of my babyhood, passively mobile in an ample pram, or in the imagined experience of travelling in cosy railway sleeping cars and the cabins of luxury liners, I felt in the other garden that I had gone on a perceptible (if spatially infinitesimal) journey without forfeiting the protection and comfort of home. My father, who hated holidays and was bored by 'abroad', may have recovered a vestige of the same infantile satisfaction when he habitually surrendered to *wanderlust* in the early afternoon with no risk of missing his lunch.

At the lower end of the other garden, the wall was pierced by a wrought-iron gate. This opened on to a flight of steps, with ramshackle greenhouses on either side, ending in a footpath which led at right angles to a narrow street known as Love's Lane. Beneath the path, behind a brief fringe of turf, stood Love's Cottage – thought to be the oldest surviving dwelling-place in the village. Top-heavily thatched and emphatically half-timbered, with low beams, an enormous open fireplace and an outside Elsan, it was picturesque and primitive enough to satisfy the most romantic taste for 'period' discomfort. This taste had not been shared by its last occupant, an elderly bachelor who had worked as a gardener for the previous owners before retiring to one of the new council houses going up along the Swindon road.

My parents had left Love's Cottage empty for some years, and then they offered to lend it throughout the spring and summer months to an old friend of my father's family, an impoverished widow who had once been famous as 'the beautiful Mrs Bassett'. Of Mr Bassett, little was known and less remembered: people sometimes asked incurious questions about him and received frank answers which they immediately forgot. Since the 1890s Dodo Bassett had been the *maîtresse en titre* of a distinguished General, whose wife steadfastly refused to give him a divorce, and a mild scandal had been caused during the First World War by the conspicuous presence of Dodo among his entourage during his visits to the Front. The General had recently died when Dodo began to spend from May to September of every year at Love's Cottage.

She must have been sixty, but her beauty still blazed: buttercup hair; long eyes that seemed as soft as purple pansies; generously curving lips that never quite ceased to smile. These features were often partly hidden by the wide brim of a picture hat, which she wore at a slant to cover one side of her face and around which an admirer had to peer in order to enjoy an uninterrupted view. She had lost her figure decades ago, but it didn't really matter; that mysterious deep bosom, with no visible cleft, which vaguely and not ungracefully merged into a comfortable stomach and rolling hips, only added to her womanly glamour. Dodo indeed was womanliness incarnate, in the sense that her Edwardian contemporaries had given to the word: sweet and warm as a bower, apparently slightly scatter-brained yet assumed to be essentially wise.

I was nearly thirteen when I first knew her. Intrigued by

11

her worldliness and reassured by her conventionality, I responded to her gently ruthless pursuit of pleasure with recognition, surprise and delight. Sometimes I would find her sitting on a deck-chair in the other garden, calmly rereading her signed copy of *Under Five Reigns* by Lady Dorothy Nevill. Often she would arrive to visit my parents, panting slightly after the short climb, bringing with her a scrap of harmless gossip for their entertainment. She had the hedonist's magic power of dignifying the most tentative sortie with the excitement of an outing and of transforming the tamest indulgence into a special treat.

We both spent much of our time scheming to find a way of getting into Marlborough, which although only a distance of ten miles from our village was not easily accessible as Dodo had never ridden a bicycle or learnt to drive a car. If we failed to wangle a free lift we would make the journey together by bus. Once in the town, Dodo would head for W. H. Smith's in the hope of finding the latest issue of one of her favourite magazines: *Vogue*, *Harper's Bazaar*, the *Tatler*, the *Sketch*, the *Bystander* or the *Sporting and Dramatic News*. We would then cross the broad High Street to settle in at the Polly Tea Rooms for scones and jam and Devonshire cream. The feeling of sickness which this feast invariably produced in me, soon to be augmented by a headache as I tried to read the glossy pages of Dodo's magazine on the jolting homeward bus, seemed so intrinsic a part of the pleasure jaunt that it scarcely counted as pain.

Occasionally, after tea, Dodo and I would stay on in Marlborough to attend the 'six o'clock house' at the cinema a few steps away from the Polly. One of the first films that we saw there was *Dodsworth*, starring Ruth Chatterton, Walter Huston and Mary Astor. I knew that she knew that it was a type of movie considered 'unsuitable' for me, but this was an impediment to enjoyment that she superbly ignored. Dodo was in fact particularly anxious to see it because one of the minor parts was played by David

12

Niven, at that time still in his twenties and not yet widely known. Although Dodo had never actually met David Niven, she had been an acquaintance of his mother's and took a keen interest in his career, on which she was remarkably well informed. She told me that he had distinguished himself by passing brilliantly out of Sandhurst but that later he had impulsively left the army to seek his fortune in Hollywood. During his scenes in *Dodsworth* she leant forward to watch him intently, and appeared to be pleased by what she saw. I felt that (as at Sandhurst) he had satisfied some exacting standard set by an expert judge, and that Dodo had awarded him full marks not only for acting ability and for good looks but also for some other quality which I could not define but of which she was an acknowledged connoisseur.

The following year, we went again to the cinema in Marlborough. 'It's an English thing called *The Vagabond Heart*,' Dodo explained beforehand at the Polly, 'and I don't expect it will be much of a film. But I hear that the son of a friend of mine has a tiny part in it and I'm curious to see how he's turned out.'

'Do you mean David Niven?'

'No, no, this is another one. Sybil Demarest's boy. I knew her pretty well at one time – we often used to run across each other at Biarritz – but that was years ago and we've quite lost touch. She had this *very* handsome son called Sandy. He was only a little boy when I saw him last, but I often come across his photograph in magazines. He made quite a name for himself as an amateur jockey – I'm not sure he didn't win the Grand National one year. But poor old Charlie Demarest came a cropper in the Crash, like so many others, and I suppose Sandy needed to make some money, so he went on the stage. Purely on the strength of his looks – I'm told that he can't act for toffee. He doesn't really belong with the theatrical crowd, you see, more in the horsey set.'

The opening credits to *The Vagabond Heart* did not

13

include Sandy Demarest. Dodo seemed puzzled. 'Perhaps he uses another name when he acts,' she said. 'Yes, I expect that's it.' She was proved right about the film not being up to much, but our attention was held throughout by the possibility of Sybil Demarest's good-looking son putting in a sudden, brief appearance. Whenever a male figure not easily identifiable as one of the leading players entered the aimlessly episodic story, Dodo would say, 'There he is! ... No, I don't think it can be ... No, that wasn't him after all. How odd.' At the end of the movie, we stayed in our seats to watch while a list of the entire cast was shown on the screen. The very last character mentioned was 'Man in night club ... Alexander Demarest.'

'Oh dear, what a pity, we must have missed him,' said Dodo resignedly. 'I don't remember a scene in a night club, do you? Well, I know I'll never be able to sit through that silly film again, so there we are.'

But only a week or so after this disappointment, Dodo came to have tea with my parents in a state of unusual animation. 'Such an extraordinary coincidence! I thought I'd go for a stroll along by the river – you know, that part that's so lovely, down near the Manor gates – and I was standing on the bridge looking at the water in a sort of day-dream, when I heard a voice just beside me say, "That's never the Bassett Hound!" I nearly jumped out of my skin – nobody's called me that for ages! And who do you think was standing there? Sybil Demarest – quite a ghost from the past, as far as I was concerned, and I must have seemed the same to her. I assumed at first that she was staying at the Manor, but no. "Hadn't you heard?" she said. "Charlie's taken Watermead." That's that sweet little house tucked away right down on the river, about a mile from the village. One can't reach it by road, only by a path through the fields ... Anyway, I walked back with her as far as Watermead and then came straight on here. I said I was longing to hear all her news, and she did tell me a bit about what has happened to her since I saw her last – so I'm

14

afraid I'm still quite full of it!'

Nothing much, as it turned out, *had* happened to Sandy's mother during that interval, and to judge from Dodo's account the Demarests were an unremarkable couple. However, one aspect of their circumstances did constitute a departure – if rather a tepid one – from the conventional norm: although living together as husband and wife, they were in fact divorced. 'Sybil was a beauty, you see, could have married almost anyone, and we were all a bit surprised when she settled for Charlie. He'd made a fortune on the Stock Exchange and he simply worshipped the ground she trod on, so when after a time she got fed up he agreed to a separation, and eventually gave her a divorce, but still went on being incredibly generous. People did think it a bit hard on him, I seem to remember, but one heard that he didn't mind anything so long as they stayed on friendly terms. Then, out of the blue, he *lost* all his money – or most of it, people never lose it *quite* all, do they? He just couldn't afford to go on supporting her *and* himself in the way they'd grown used to, and as she hadn't remarried they thought the most sensible thing to do was to get back together again. For part of the time, at least: they still have separate flats in London – quite tiny, she tells me – but spend their summers together down here. Rather a romantic story, in a funny sort of way, isn't it? Sybil says she shudders to *think* what the stuffy county neighbours would say if they knew that technically she and Charlie were living in sin! They're both coming to tea with me at the Cottage on Wednesday. Can I bring them up here afterwards for a moment? I'd love you all to meet.'

Sybil Demarest materialized on Wednesday afternoon wearing a smart suit of heather-coloured tweed and a green felt pork-pie hat with a pheasant's feather stuck in the brim. She was a few years younger than Dodo and her beauty was of a less showy type: round pale blue eyes, delicate features and a small, prissy mouth. Her fair hair, faintly greying, was parted in the middle, gently waved and loosely knotted at her neck. Unlike Dodo, she gave the impression of intending to 'grow old gracefully'. Her husband was more than a little deaf, which may have partly explained the worried and irritable look that seldom left his aquiline, rather haggard countenance. His body was spare, compact and beginning to be slightly bent; he had an impatient, clipped way of talking and seemed to be continually on the watch for some anticipated offence against propriety – some breach, however minor, of the rules which he believed should govern correct social behaviour.

The conversation started with a tentative analysis of current affairs. 'What price the Nazis, eh?' Mr Demarest asked.

'The only one that I've got any time for,' said his wife, 'is Field-Marshal Goering. I hope this doesn't sound too fearfully snobbish, but I'm told on good authority that he's what we used to call a gentleman by birth. Which is more than can be said for Herr Hitler.' Sybil had a low, musical voice and spoke in measured, stately tones.

Charlie nodded. 'Don't know whether I'd agree about his being a gent, but he's certainly a damned fine sportsman. Man at my club I sometimes play cards with tells me he's never come across a better shot. Best of a bad bunch, if you ask me.'

'But I don't care much for his looks, do you?' said Dodo. 'I always think a good figure is every bit as important in a man as in a woman.'

'Dear lady, we are not discussing a beauty competition,' said Charlie. 'We are contemplating the possibility of war.'

'Oh no!' cried Dodo. 'I don't think I could stand another one!'

'Personally,' said Sybil, 'I think all this talk about a war is quite unnecessary, rather irresponsible and, what is more, extremely dangerous. People panic so easily – just like sheep. But if it should be decreed in Heaven – or in Hell, or wherever – that there is to be one, well then, so be it, say I.

16

Mind you, I speak as someone who has already been through two wars. I see no reason why I should consider myself incapable of surviving a third.'

'Oh do let's change the subject!' said Dodo. 'How is dear Sandy? I saw that he won another race not long ago, before the flat season started. He *has* done well for himself, hasn't he?'

The faces of both the Demarests altered at the sound of the name. Charlie's frown of angry concern smoothed and his mouth twisted into a reluctant, reminiscent smile; Sybil's self-consciously noble expression softened to one of doting indulgence.

'He'll be down here soon, I've no doubt,' said Mr Demarest. 'Can't keep away from the river for long. Though I say so myself, that boy of mine is no mean dry fly fisherman. I thought *I* knew how to use a rod until he grew up and started to show his poor old father what was what.'

'Oh yes, he spends every *second* he can spare at Watermead,' said Sybil. 'But at the moment he's frantically busy filming and I don't know when he'll be able to get away.'

Dodo was tactfully silent about *The Vagabond Heart*. 'I saw him in that very amusing play with Gertrude Lawrence ... didn't I?' she ventured.

'Indeed, yes,' said Sybil. 'Darling Gertie is a very close friend of Sandy's and tries to get a part for him in all her shows.'

'*What* an attractive girl!' said Dodo. 'I'd love to know her secret. She's got no looks, strictly speaking, but *such* charm, and that's half the battle, isn't it?'

Charlie grunted. 'She turns herself out well – I'll give her that.'

Sybil Demarest looked grave. 'Do you know the thing about Gertie that I admire most? It may surprise you, but I'll tell you just the same.' She paused. 'That woman is the *cleanest* creature it has ever been my good fortune to meet. Yes ... I would be perfectly happy to eat a poached egg off any part of Gertrude Lawrence's body!' She paused again, to savour the effect of her words; but, finding our response to them inadequate, felt that she had to continue. 'And on top of that, she's got what I can only call a hell of a lot of guts! She hasn't a nerve in her anatomy! Jeepers *creepers*, how I envy her!'

'I *would* love to meet your son,' said my mother. 'Do bring him to see us when he's next here.'

'How extremely kind of you,' said Sybil coldly. 'I shall certainly give him your message but I'm afraid I'm not able to offer you very much hope. His days here are so deeply precious to him that any time *not* spent in the open air what I call flogging the water counts as time wasted for Sandy.'

This speech was succeeded by a silence which gave everybody full opportunity to take in its insulting implications. After a few seconds Sybil's face showed that she had taken them in herself; she appeared to hesitate on the brink of making some kind of apology; but, realizing that this would only confirm and compound her bad manners, she rose instead to leave.

'I can see we're never going to be allowed to get so much as a *peep* at Sandy!' said Dodo indignantly after the Demarests had gone. 'How *silly* of Sybil to try to keep him tied to her apron strings like that! It's always a mistake – I've known so many cases. What was that thing – *The Silver Cord* – such an unpleasant play, but damnably clever ... It's such hard lines on *him*, that's what gets my goat.'

By now Dodo's desire to lay eyes on Sandy Demarest had spread not only to my mother but also to the rest of us. His link (however tenuous) with stage and screen made him an object of interest to me; and even my father, having heard Sandy's horsemanship highly praised as well as repeated rumours of the young man's unusual good looks, declared himself curious to see this modern Adonis in the flesh. My mother defiantly resolved to find some method of getting past Sybil Demarest's guard and scraping an acquaintance with her son. Then, one day, Dodo reported that, while standing on the same bridge that had witnessed her reunion with Sybil, she had caught sight of a tall male figure in waders fishing in a distant reach of the river. 'I'm quite sure it wasn't old Charlie – this was a much younger man. Bet you anything it was Sandy! And I happen to know that Sybil's away in Newmarket, visiting an old flame of hers who trains up there and who, as a matter of fact, used to be quite a flirt of *mine*.'

'Right!' said my mother. 'What's to prevent me from ringing up Mr Demarest straight away and inviting him to a very small and informal and last-minute cocktail party this evening and asking him to bring whoever else is staying in the house? If I take him by surprise, it might just work.' She walked determinedly to the telephone, and could soon be heard talking slowly and very loudly to the deaf Charlie. After a short conversation, she hung up.

'*What* did he say?' Dodo eagerly demanded.

'It's really rather funny – but the joke's on us. He can't manage tonight, but he'd simply love to look in around tea-time tomorrow. Sandy's leaving first thing in the morning so would it be all right if he brought his daughter Kay with him? Of course I said "yes". Did you know there was a daughter too?'

'First I've heard of her,' said Dodo.

So Charlie Demarest paid us a second pointless call. As before, he gruffly volunteered a series of civil banalities in a manner which suggested that any response to them would be unwelcome (because inaudible) and might easily cause him to lose his temper. This inhibited the smooth flow of social intercourse, creating a 'sticky' situation in no way lubricated by his daughter who, beyond a few muttered pleasantries, hardly spoke at all.

Kay Demarest was then in her early thirties. She wore no make-up, which gave her a prematurely weatherbeaten appearance; her reddish hair hung to her shoulders in a long untidy bob; she was extremely thin. Her evident

19

shyness gave her a hunted look, the gauche grace of a deer who senses danger but is uncertain of the exact quarter from which it threatens. She had her mother's large, sad aquamarine eyes in her father's narrow, ascetic face; also like her father was the way in which her apprehensive expression (a less fierce, more vulnerable version of his) could on rare occasions of confidence or amusement relax into a crooked, rueful smile of considerable charm. She had on a tartan shirt, brown corduroy bell-bottom slacks and high-heeled shoes which seemed to hurt her (perhaps because she wore neither stockings nor socks); she carried a big, battered handbag (made of some expensive skin such as alligator or crocodile but now split and wrinkled like a stretch of parched and pallid desert) to which she clung as though for reassurance, while with an air of secretive concentration she chain-smoked throughout the visit.

To me there was a mystery almost as fascinating as Greta Garbo's in Kay's offhand behaviour, laconic speech and deliberately shabby clothes, but she was also the reverse of intimidating and I found in her an attractive combination of the cosy and the strange. When she shook hands with me to say goodbye, she unexpectedly added a few hesitant words to the formal valediction. 'To tell you the truth, I was scared stiff of this tea party. I nearly funked it, but Daddy made me come. I thought you'd all be simply terrifying, but you're not. You've been sweet. I like the atmosphere here – I feel I can be myself.' She had been speaking with head averted, but now she turned to face me and I saw those enormous eyes, of a blue both pale and piercing, in the lean, bony face. 'Thank you'.

II

That autumn, I was as usual a few days late going back to the public school where I had already spent three bewildered, anxious terms. My dread of the holiday's end invariably lent me sufficient will power during its last hours to send my temperature the necessary degrees above normal to qualify as an official invalid – but I could never keep it up for long enough to win more than a tantalizingly brief remission. Hopes of a further reprieve were temporarily raised by the Munich crisis, in which I perceived a promising possibility that the school might be bombed, or in some other way put out of action by war. One of my few friends there was a boy called Billy Phipps, who was a year older than myself and whose worldly experience impressed me though I was often offended by the implacable snobbery of the conclusions he had drawn from it. He thought that to be *petit bourgeois* was so disgraceful as to be almost obscene, and while he loved to analyse this dreaded state and its various tell-tale manifestations he could hardly bring himself to mention them by name and had therefore constructed a set of euphemistic codes by which to refer to them. 'MC' for 'middle class' was comparatively easy to decipher, but 'K' (facetiously standing for 'common') and 'NQOCD' ('not quite our class darling') were impenetrable to the uninitiated – and the cryptic acronym 'MIF' retained some of its mystery even after one had been told that it was an abbreviation of 'milk in first'.

There were several grounds on which I was resentfully obliged to acknowledge myself inferior to Billy Phipps, and the fact that these tended to be social rather than moral or intellectual did not make the admission less humiliating. For example, his wide circle of acquaintance made me feel as if I and my parents knew hardly anyone at all, passing our lives uneasily in a pathetic and slightly sinister void. In an attempt to imply that our isolation might not be total, I mentioned to Billy that the Demarests had recently become our neighbours and was pleased to find that this piece of news not only caught his attention but was even greeted with wary approval. His aunt was a successful breeder of race horses and a well-known figure at the smarter meetings, so Billy was familiar with the subtleties of that world and considered himself an authority on its totems and taboos.

'How did you get on with Sandy?' he asked. 'My aunt says he can be very good company when he feels like it.'

I told him that I had not yet met Sandy but that I knew his sister slightly. Like Dodo, Billy Phipps had never heard of Kay, suggesting by his manner of saying so that he suspected me of having invented or imagined her. After the Christmas holidays, however, he condescendingly confirmed her existence. 'I asked my aunt about your friends the Demarests,' he said, 'and you're perfectly right, Sandy does have a sister. But I gather she's rather *mal vu* on the race course. Doesn't go down at all well, I'm afraid.'

With some vague notion that Kay might have been 'warned off the turf', like the hero of *The Calendar* by Edgar Wallace, I asked him what he meant.

'She's supposed to sleep with jockeys,' Billy explained. 'Mind you, my aunt says that there may not be a word of truth in it – but once a girl gets that sort of reputation, she's done.'

'What else did your aunt say about the Demarests?'

'Parents *très ordinaires* – Stockbroker Surrey, if you know what I mean, though there is a theory that the father comes from an old Huguenot family and I believe the mother has some quite respectable Norfolk connections ... As for Sandy, opinion seems to be divided. My aunt says of course he's much too pretty for his own good but he can be *so* amusing that one forgives him a lot. At first you think he must be either a roaring pansy or a poodle-faking gigolo – you know, the type of chap one's Nanny might describe as "Good-looking – *and* knows it!" – but my aunt says no, that's not fair, *other men like him*, and my aunt says that's always an infallible sign in a fellow that there's nothing really the matter with him.'

I repeated a part of this to my parents and to Dodo, but something made me suppress the malicious remarks about Kay.

The following summer, I saw her again. I had set out early one afternoon on an aimless walk: through the other garden, past Dodo's cottage and down Love's Lane to the main street of the village. Kay was standing at the bottom of the lane, a bulky square black box on the pavement beside her. When I reached the street I recognized the box as a portable wind-up gramophone.

'I say,' said Kay, 'you wouldn't do me the most tremendous favour, would you, and help me with this thing? I was so afraid it was bust for good, and then my friend Reg at the garage was terribly sweet and saved my life by repairing it for nothing, but I'd quite forgotten it was so damned heavy and I'm not sure I can lug it all the way back home by myself.'

Of course I said I would be delighted to carry her gramophone, and we started off together down the street. 'We'll take it in turns,' she said. 'I absolutely insist on that because it's quite a long way, so promise to call out as soon as you begin to feel exhausted ... Listen, would it drive you mad if I popped for a moment into the paper shop? There's something rather important I've got to collect there.' She emerged from the shop with the latest issue of a weekly film magazine. 'Sorry to be such an awful bore, but can you bear to wait just one more second while I find out if they've printed a letter I sent them?'

With urgent concentration, Kay leafed through the magazine, but failed to find what she wanted. 'To tell you the truth,' she said, as we continued on our journey, 'I'm beginning to get a bit fed up with George of *Picturegoer*. I'm beginning to wonder if he isn't really rather a swindle. You know, he boasts that he can answer *any* question – within reason, of course – that a reader puts to him. He guarantees to publish your request plus his answer within a month of receiving it. That is, unless you want to keep the whole thing private, in which case you enclose a stamped addressed envelope ... Well, it must be more than six weeks now since I sent in a perfectly straightforward query – which has been greeted with dead silence! I seem to have totally stumped him. Too pathetic!'

'What did you ask him?'

'The date of Tyrone Power's birthday. As simple as that.'

'Why do you want to know his age?'

'I don't – I want to know his astrological sign. So that I can cast his horoscope. I saw him in a thing called *Rose of Washington Square* and thought he was the most attractive man I've ever seen, that's why. It's a good picture, too. If it's ever showing anywhere near you, for God's sake, take my advice and go. I can thoroughly recommend it. I should be very surprised indeed if it disappointed you.'

We had now come to the end of the village and instead of continuing along the main thoroughfare, which would have taken us past the Manor gates in the direction of Marlborough, we turned left down a minor road and crossed a bridge over the river. Just as the ground was steepening, at the bottom of Larch Hill, Kay led me over a stile and into a field on the right. The path to Watermead took us through further fields and meadows which became increasingly soggy underfoot. Some gates could be opened but others had to be climbed over, under or through. The house was hidden from the path by tall bushes; an almost invisible gap in one of these admitted us on to a sloping croquet lawn. The building was low, of two storeys, and gave the impression of leaning solicitously over the river – a tiny tributary of which flowed beneath the rooms at the back. Life at Watermead, I was later to learn, unfolded to a constant accompaniment of varying liquid sounds – trickling, roaring, bubbling, lapping – which suggested to the spirit an endless alternation of refreshment and erosion.

'You've simply got to come inside and recover,' said Kay. 'The very least I can do in return for your kindness is to offer you a cup of tea! Don't worry, it's quite safe, the coast's clear. Mummy's with her boyfriend in Newmarket, thank God – long may she remain there, though I suppose I shouldn't say so – and Daddy won't be back for hours, so we shan't have to make polite conversation.'

I said that I didn't want any tea but would love to listen to something on her gramophone.

'Would you really? I used to have rather a good collection of records but most of them either got broken or are scattered around the country – I've moved about a lot in the past few years, you see. But I've clung on to a few precious favourites. They're up in my bedroom. Make yourself comfortable in here while I go and fetch them.'

She showed me into a long, dim sitting-room furnished with Knole sofas, chintz-covered armchairs and rickety round occasional tables fretted to a vaguely Oriental design. The walls were hung with glass cases containing stuffed trout, each one captioned by details of its weight and date of death, between a series of small casement windows with mullioned panes; the floor was uneven, and perceptibly lower at the farther end. Two framed photographs stood on the mantelpiece, one of Sybil Demarest *en profil perdu* and the other of Queen Marie of Romania, the sitter's face almost obliterated by her signature; next to these I noticed the glossy calendar sent out to their clients by Ladbroke the bookmakers, with a flattering caricature of some racing celebrity for every month. The room satisfied an undemanding standard of impersonal comfort, neither repelling nor absorbing the visitor, and I felt as if I had been left on an empty stage in a scene set to represent the lounge of a typically English country hotel. The continual murmur of moving water around and below me seemed as illusory as a theatrical 'special effect' while I waited – both audience and actor – for the play to begin.

Kay returned with an armful of records and we both crouched by the gramophone while she wound it up. Just the sight of the labels was enough to put me in a party mood – smart Parlophone in deep blue and white, festive Vocalion in bright red and gold, sober Brunswick in understated black. It was apparent that the tunes preferred by Kay were torch songs: she played me Connee Boswell singing 'Say It Isn't So', Ruth Etting singing 'Lost – a Heart as Good as New', Alice Faye singing 'There's a Lull in My Life', Helen Morgan singing 'Why Was I Born?' But the despairing lyrics and sensuous, sedated *tempi* did not strike me then as depressing. They seemed rather to convey, in an inviting form, the essence of a distant, adult world of melodrama – a world from which Kay, for reasons as yet mysterious, had decided for a while to retire. I had fantasies, as we listened to the luridly defeatist music, of Kay having been forced to 'hide out' like a gangster's moll at Watermead, for there was certainly something furtive and temporary about her manner of inhabiting this inhospitable house.

'Why did you say that you thought we'd be frightening, when we first met last summer?' I asked her before I left.

'Oh – nothing personal. It's just that I'd understood that your parents were friends of *my* parents, and for as long as I can remember the sort of people that Daddy and Mummy approve of have invariably made me feel hopelessly inadequate, to the point where I just sit there tongue-tied like an idiot. But I soon realized that your family aren't like that at all ... Talking of which, Mummy will be back in a day or two and it looks as if this lovely sunny spell we're having might last a bit longer. I wonder if you'd do me another great favour and give your mother a message from me? Would she be angelic and let me borrow just a corner of your garden to sun-bathe in? I wouldn't be any trouble – no one need know I'm there. It's just that I adore the sun, but seeing me lie about all day half-naked gets on Mummy's nerves. She's bound to complain to Daddy sooner or later, and then all hell will break loose and my life here won't be worth living.'

'Of course I'll ask her and I'm sure she'll be delighted for you to use the garden whenever you like ... But, when you have a row with your parents as you've just described, doesn't your brother take your side?'

'Sandy? Oh, poor lamb, I wouldn't want to involve *him* in one of those ghastly scenes. It would only make him miserable. Besides, he's hardly ever here.'

So, while the fine weather lasted, Kay would turn up regularly around noon, wearing shorts and a shirt and carrying a car rug which she would spread on a patch of lawn at a tactful distance from the house. After removing her shirt, she would tie her headscarf round her bosom – thus freeing her untidy mane of copper-coloured hair. Surrounded by bottles of sun-tan oil, packets of cigarettes and books of matches, a recent number of *Picturegoer* and a paper bag containing sandwiches and a chocolate bar, with a battery wireless hissing and mumbling near her head, she would lie almost motionless with eyes closed in ecstasy until the evening chill. When she turned on her front, she would untie the scarf, and if she shifted her position once again her small breasts would be briefly revealed, pale round vulnerable patches in the dark brown of her body.

There was something paradoxically unhealthy about the intensity of Kay's sun-worship. Her skin acquired an unpleasantly leathery texture as its tan deepened; the effort of so dedicated a surrender to passive immobility seemed to be draining her of all vitality. Occasionally, she would join my family indoors for a drink at the end of the day; more often, she would creep or stagger back home, like an early morning reveller sated but befuddled after a night of dissipation. She soon struck up a friendship with my mother, who was nearly as intrigued by her as I was; but my father, although he hid the feeling, did not really like her. Her lack of the more conventional social graces made him uncomfortable; he found her air of self-absorption an irritant and a bore. It was therefore lucky that Kay instinctively refrained from choosing a site for her sun-bathing activities in the other garden.

In the end, the meeting with Sandy which had been so eagerly desired the previous summer came about quite naturally through the mediation of Kay. She telephoned my mother one August afternoon. 'I've got my brother here on a flying visit and he says he's heard so much about you all that he simply must know you. Do you think we could possibly come round straight away?' I ran with the news down to Dodo's cottage, and she followed me back to the house. But the excitement of the year before was lacking; the period of waiting had been too long for it to survive, and I think we may even have felt that there had been something slightly silly about the fuss over Sandy that we had been ready to make then. So his eventual appearance – though not exactly a disappointment – was inevitably an anti-climax.

My mother and Dodo and I were sitting on the front lawn just outside the house (my father had absented himself to the other garden) when Kay turned in at the drive accompanied by a tall dark-haired man in his late twenties. She walked towards us with the tarty gait that she affected when she was happy, swinging her hips and shoulders and taking slow, deliberate steps. 'I'll never be able to introduce you properly – he's been making me laugh too much!' she said, collapsing on to the grass beside me. 'But anyway, this is Sandy!'

28

Billy Phipps's aunt had been inaccurate when she described Sandy as 'pretty': his good looks were rather of the gentle but decidedly masculine type exemplified by Gary Cooper, which often appear to be a burden to their owner and are worn with an air of apologetic diffidence. In Sandy's case, one felt that he would have liked to ignore them but that circumstances had somehow made this impossible. His lanky body moved with hesitant caution instead of the ease expected of an athlete, and the geometrically regular features in his long, grave face were troubled by an apprehensive expression at odds with the confident charm of his social manner. There was something stagily synthetic about this manner, as if it had been assumed in order to allay suspicion of narcissistic conceit without going to the tedious extreme of crude virility; perhaps as a result of the strain involved in adhering to this middle course, the total effect of his personality contained a surprising suggestion of asexuality. As some young men are said to have 'outgrown their strength', so Sandy seemed to have been subtly emasculated by his own beauty.

'Yes, the dear girl had a frightful attack of the giggles just outside the Post Office and I'm sorry to say made rather an exhibition of herself,' he explained. 'I even feared for a moment that she was going to "do herself a mischief". God knows what it was that she found so funny – I merely told her a very old and rather asinine joke. Quite unrepeatable, I'm afraid,' he added firmly.

'It was the way you told it ... But we were laughing before then.'

'You mean, the Football Club game? They'll think us *quite* mad if we tell them about that ... You must forgive us, you see, but my sister and I suffer from an extremely infantile sense of humour. The Football Club game is really very simple – literally anyone can play it! You just imagine the club as a married couple of title, being announced by a butler at some very grand party. Sir Aston and Lady Villa,

29

for example – can't you just see them? Kay's favourite is Sir Woolwich and Lady Arsenal.' Sandy assumed an accent like Noël Coward's to add, 'What did you think of the Arsenals? ... Loved him, hated her!'

Within a few minutes of his arrival, he had us all merrily competing at the Football Club game. Its possibilities, however, were soon exhausted – and there followed a pause in which, though it remained unuttered, we seemed to hear the sweet, silly cry of the spoiled child: 'What shall we play next?' Dodo had brought with her a capacious sewing bag, patterned with green and yellow storks on a black background, which contained no sewing but was filled instead with cosmetic accessories; this bag had now companionably subsided in a colourful spread at her feet. Spotting a copy of the *Tatler* obtruding from its open clasp, Sandy squatted beside her deck-chair. 'May I?' he asked, smiling up at her as he extracted the magazine. Opening it at the page devoted to photographs of recent marriages, he informed her in a conspiratorial half-whisper of the rules of another 'game'. One had to guess from the wedding pictures (beaming brides wreathed in orange blossom, sheepish grooms in tails or braided uniforms) at the quality of each couple's love life. 'This pair, three or four times a night, I'd say, at least to start with, wouldn't you? But these with the Guard of Honour – oh dear, once a month at *most!*' Dodo was flattered and amused by his attention, but she was also offended and annoyed. She gave a repressive shake of her head and, glancing at me, muttered, '*Pas devant...*' Almost snatching the *Tatler* from his hands, she replaced it in her bag – withdrawing from its depths a copy of *Gone with the Wind*.

'Isn't it disgraceful?' she said. 'I've been reading this religiously ever since it came out *donkey's* years ago and I still haven't finished it! Mind you, I'm loving every word of it – but I just can't seem to get to the end!'

Sandy made a mock-penitent grimace in rueful acknowledgment of misbehaviour, and smoothly adapted to the change of topic by giving us an inside account of the circumstances surrounding the casting of Scarlett O'Hara in the film version of Dodo's book. This led on to other enjoyable theatrical anecdotes. When Sandy referred to 'Larry and Viv' or 'Noël and Gertie' he did not seem to be dropping names in the vulgar cause of self-promotion; such allusions to the famous were camouflaged, as it were, by more frequent mentions of less easily identifiable diminutives – Betty and Bobby and Boots and Babs – belonging to actors and actresses as obscure as himself. Nearly all his stories centred on some on-stage disaster which had befallen him or one of his friends. Sandy's underpants had dropped to his ankles and tripped him up while he was carrying a spear in *Julius Caesar* when the Duke and Duchess of Gloucester were in the audience; Babs, after years as an understudy, had finally landed the lead in *Hedda* at Scunthorpe rep, only to 'corpse' on the line about vine leaves in Ejlert Lövborg's hair; poor Bobby suffered so severely from stage fright that on a famous occasion he had let off a fart in the middle of the Messenger scene in *Antony and Cleopatra*. While he spoke, Kay listened in silence, neither watching him directly nor laughing at his jokes, but with an expression on her face of the deepest content.

'How is your dear mother?' Dodo asked. 'I don't seem to have seen her around much lately.'

'The Head Woman?' said Sandy. 'She Who Must Be Obeyed? It's quite all right, she knows the rude names I call her. As a matter of fact, I think she rather likes them ... She's staying with friends in Scotland. Left last night. Coming back in a month.'

'Which will be a signal for *me* to make a move,' Kay murmured so that only I could hear. 'I can just about cope with Daddy on his own, but I'm afraid the two of them together rather get me down.'

'Where will you go?'

'Not sure yet,' she replied evasively. 'Brighton, possibly.

31

I'll find somewhere.'

During this muted exchange, Dodo had started to reminisce about the old days, when she and Sybil had first been friends. 'One episode I remember in particular – so killingly funny, it was, we always laugh about it when we meet – I *don't* think she'd mind my telling you. There was some new fad that was supposed to be frightfully good for one, and very rejuvenating and all that, called the Garlic Cure. One just ate nothing but garlic for days on end – it cleaned out the system, or something. Anyway, I had a little place in the Cotswolds then, and I said to Sybil, why don't you come down and stay with me and we'll give it a try together? *Too* boring on one's own, you see. So there we were, my dear, perfectly happy, having eaten *not one thing* that wasn't garlic for an entire weekend and no doubt smelling to high heaven (we didn't notice it ourselves, because one doesn't) when to our *horror* one afternoon we looked out of the window and saw two horsemen come riding up to the front door! It was two rather special beaux of ours – the Merton twins, Jumbo and Boy – who were in the neighbourhood and thought they'd give us a nice surprise by calling unexpectedly! Well, of course, there was no *question* of letting them in! We just stood at the window shrieking "Go *away*! Go *away*!" In the end they did, but they must have thought us completely bats!'

Throughout Dodo's story Sandy stood beside her chair, bending a little towards her in order to hear every word, his brown eyes blank and his upper lip slightly raised in a politely appreciative smirk, frozen in preparation for the long-delayed release into loud laughter which only the end of the anecdote would permit. When this happened, Kay spoke again, still in a low voice as though addressing herself as much as me. 'How spooky ... I was watching Sandy while she was talking and I suddenly had a sort of vision. I suddenly saw *exactly* how he'll look when he's very, very old. So now I know what he'll be like then ...'

Dodo then rose, and said she must return to her cottage; Sandy and Kay offered to escort her there, on their way back to Watermead; the little party broke up. While Sandy was bidding my mother goodbye, he suddenly leant forward and gave her an impulsive kiss. 'That's to thank you for being so sweet and kind to our darling Kay!' he said.

A week or so later, war was declared. On the following day, I met Kay coming out of the paper shop in the village. She called out to me, 'Guess what! At *last*! George of *Picturegoer* has answered my question! I can't think what took him so long, but better late than never. Power was born on May 5th, which makes him a Taurus. I had a feeling he might be.'

'Isn't the news awful?' I said.

Kay seemed to flinch. 'The war, you mean?' she muttered, clearly at a loss as to how to react to my remark. I wondered for a moment if I had ignorantly flouted some tacit code of wartime behaviour which forbade any direct reference to the war itself. Then, with a mixture of her father's curt authority and her mother's complacent inanity, but redeemed for me by a touch of the gruff bravado that I had come to recognize as peculiarly hers, she announced, 'I give it a month!'

III

I can't remember exactly how soon it was after the outbreak of war that work began on the building of a large military aerodrome along the top of Larch Hill – above the village and just out of sight from it – but it must have taken some considerable time because I'm sure that it wasn't finished until the spring of 1941. By then I had left school and was hanging about at home waiting to go up to Oxford for a year or two of further study before the inevitable Army call-up. In the meantime, I had joined the Home Guard. One of my weirdest duties was to spend a night on this aerodrome – recently completed but not yet operational – with only one other Home Guard private, presumably in order to defend it from the possible threat of attack. My companion was Harry Vokins, a boy of my own age (nearly seventeen) who lived above the village paper shop. Neither of us understood whether the Government property we had been ordered to protect was thought to be in danger from German forces or merely vulnerable to mischievous local vandalism – and, if the former, whether enemy approach should be expected by land or from the air. Obediently but uncertainly, dressed in our baggy, prickly uniforms and armed with gas masks and rifles, we climbed the hill at eight o'clock in the evening to start our twelve hours' vigil.

As a small child, my fantasies of flight had centred on this hill and its peak had symbolized the limit of my infantile horizon. One winter, when the house was full of guests for

Christmas, I had been moved upstairs from my night nursery on the first floor to an attic bedroom, and from its unfamiliar window (low in the room but high in the outside wall) the summit of Larch Hill had seemed almost within leaping distance – much nearer than the church and the village street and the river in the valley between us. But the fantasies always stopped short at the hilltop, ending with a gentle landing on the crest and never indulging in curiosity about what, if anything, lay beyond. And later on, as I grew older, the impression persisted that nothing in fact did lie beyond the hill, even though I often climbed its grassy slope on foot or was driven up and over it on the minor road which led away from the village to the south. This was because, once Larch Hill had been ascended, it no longer seemed to have been a hill at all; the ground imperceptibly steadied itself before settling into a flat viewless field, so lacking in drama that it could not even be described as a plain.

But now it lacked drama no longer: a silent desert of crescent-shaped hangars, brutalist huts and endless runways, of tarmac, concrete and corrugated iron, the aerodrome awaited Harry Vokins and myself on the top of the hill like an immense ghost town, spooky in a peculiarly modern – even a futuristic – way. It was of course only empty because it had not yet begun its useful life, but in the grey dusk it seemed as though it had already been abandoned by some new form of existence too sinister to survive.

We found an open hut with some camp-beds in it, and made this our headquarters. Harry had brought with him a Thermos full of tea, a chocolate cup-cake, a child's comic and a torch to read it by. I had already eaten and had forgotten to bring a book. We had been advised to share our watch by dividing it into four sections of three hours each, with one of us acting as sentry while the other slept. Harry picked the first and third periods, which meant that I was to be on duty from eleven o'clock until two in the

35

morning, and again from five o'clock until we knocked off at eight. He deposited his belongings on one of the camp-beds, then wandered out of the hut, dragging his gun behind him. I lay down on another bed but was unable to sleep. Soon I also drifted outside, where it was still faintly light. I walked around the aerodrome for nearly an hour before I came upon Harry squatting on his haunches outside a vast hollow hangar. I stood beside him and together we looked down at the blacked-out houses in the moonlit village. Neither of us spoke, until Harry amiably volunteered, 'My Gran reckons I'm stouter.'

Harry's grandmother, old Mrs Vokins, ran the paper shop; his mother, Miss Vokins, was weak in the head but a harmless and popular figure in the village; he had never known a father. Miss Vokins, who always wore black, was tall and very thin, with an impediment in her speech and a goitre; Harry resembled her in height and extreme emaciation, but he was not as simple-minded as she was although he was decidedly backward for his age. It was rumoured that he liked to expose himself to little girls in country lanes, but nothing of this kind had ever been proved against him and he was certainly incapable of inflicting physical hurt on any living creature.

Harry's gaze now shifted away from the village, following the dim glitter of the river to the left and stopping where the clump of bushes screening Watermead was darkly visible on its bank. 'But *her*,' he said, nodding his head in that direction, 'she don't agree with that, and all. No, she won't have it at any price. She reckons I'm still so skinny you could thread me through the eye of a needle, know what I mean? My Gran said she had to laugh. Oh, she's a caution, like, that Kay.'

'Oh, you mean Kay Demarest. She's a friend of mine too.'

'I run her errands for her, like,' Harry explained.

'So do I, sometimes.'

'She's a real lady,' he said, rather repressively. He rose to his feet and stretched. 'Nearly time for my kip,' he muttered, and then went off on his own. Although I had left my rifle in the hut, I decided that there was no point in following Harry back there before two o'clock, when it would be time to wake him for his second watch, so I stayed where I was and thought about Kay.

It interested but did not surprise me that Harry should turn out to be a friend of hers: so too were his rather similar contemporaries, Reg at the garage and Tom, the freckle-faced, sandy-haired boy at the Post Office whom she had nicknamed 'Spencer Tracy'. The only adult male friends whose names I had heard her mention were Roy Halma, a fortune-teller in Hove whom she regularly consulted by letter and sometimes visited in person, and Roy Halma's boyfriend Ernest, a waiter at the Old Ship Hotel in Brighton. She also corresponded with another clairvoyant to whom she just alluded as 'my sand man'. Kay would send him some trivial object which she had carried about in her handbag for a while. Clutching this in one hand, with the other the sand man would gently agitate a soup plate on which he had sprinkled a quantity of sacred grains gathered centuries ago from the Sahara Desert; within the patterns they formed, he claimed he could discern the salient aspects of Kay's immediate future.

She did have several women friends, but I had not yet succeeded in clearly establishing their names or identifying their separate personalities, because when she referred to any one of them she would do so by the inclusive term 'my girlfriend'. Such a reference usually took the form of indirect quotation, giving vehement expression to some mildly eccentric but fiercely held prejudice. 'My girlfriend refuses point blank to wear anything but silk next to her skin.' 'My girlfriend can't stand Michaelmas daisies. Won't have 'em in the house. She's just got a thing about them – they make her quite ill.' 'My girlfriend won't live north of the park. She's funny that way. Knightsbridge, Kensington, Chelsea – that's fine by her. But if somebody said to her, why don't you move to Bayswater, I'm very much afraid

37

they'd get a flea in their ear.'

Kay was equally uncommunicative about her former lovers, who also remained anonymous and whose characteristics were only hinted at. I could tell, however, that there had been a number – a married man, a man's man, a ladies' man, a gentleman jockey, an irresistible womanizer, a hopeless case, a bad lot, a good shot, a lovable shit. Some of these attributes may have coincided in the same person – but of this and other details I was never quite sure. The vagueness about facts did not irritate me, because the emotional atmosphere surrounding them was so potently evoked by Kay. Something – a snatch of song, a name glimpsed in a newspaper, a view from a window, the whistle of a train – would stir her memory; her face would assume that rueful, reminiscent, secretive expression which I had come to know well; she would mutter some barely intelligible phrase suggesting affectionate regret; and I felt that she had conveyed to me the very essence of her past relationship with a shadowy masculine image about whom I needed to know nothing more definite than that Kay had been reminded of him at that moment.

Like me, but for different reasons, Kay was now living in a kind of limbo, and our intimacy had greatly increased over the past few months, accelerated by propinquity and a shared, somewhat shameful although involuntary, désœuvrement. The war, which was causing so much misery elsewhere by separating lovers and fragmenting family life, had done the Demarests a subtler disservice: it had thrust them into undesired proximity. Fear of the Blitz had forced Sybil and Charlie to relinquish their London flats and to make Watermead their permanent and only home. Kay, too, after several sporadic and unexplained absences during the early days of the war, had reluctantly come to roost there, as it seemed for the duration. She did not want to live at Watermead and her parents did not want her to do so, but none the less there she appeared to be stuck, as if she had been officially evacuated from some danger area and billeted, against the will of all concerned, on her own family.

'I'm only there on sufferance – they make that *crystal* clear,' she had told me on one of our walks. 'What I can't stand is the way they insist on treating me as if I were still a child – they seem to forget I'll be thirty-five next birthday! They make me feel like an unclaimed parcel that has been returned to sender – in a rather battered condition! Or as if I had been let out of some prison or loony bin or other on parole, or bound over on a promise of good behaviour, or whatever the expression is. You may well ask why I put up with it. But the simple truth is, I just don't have anywhere else to go.'

So Kay, at a time when the presence of political refugees from Europe had become a familiar feature of English life, wandered round the village in search of temporary shelter as if she too had been driven into exile from the purely domestic hell of Watermead. Toting her rations in a shoulder-bag, with a once-smart scarf thrown over her head and tied beneath her chin like a peasant's shawl, she would beg to be allowed to eat her evening meal – and sometimes stay the night – at the Post Office, the garage, the paper shop or at my parents' house. 'There's such a ghastly atmosphere at home today that I just couldn't face dinner there, I'd really rather die. If I can only keep out of their way till tomorrow I'll be perfectly safe, because we're expecting Sandy back then on forty-eight hours' leave so they'll be on their best behaviour.' Sandy had enlisted in the RAF as soon as war broke out (to the distress of Charlie, who would have preferred him to have joined an old cavalry regiment) and had become a hero of the Battle of Britain.

There were people in the village who wondered why Kay did not escape from her predicament of dependence by entering one of the Women's Services or working in a munitions factory. I knew her well enough by now to understand that such obvious solutions to her problem were out of the question, although it was difficult to explain to strangers exactly why this should be the case. The self-consciousness which made her so socially maladroit in civilian life would almost certainly, in circumstances involving regimental discipline or the rigour of an assembly line, have found expression in a physical clumsiness that would have limited her usefulness and might even have constituted a potential danger. She was not, however, totally unemployable, having held down several jobs before the war, though never for very long; selling hats in a Mayfair shop called Odile, for example, and appearing as an extra in films ('One got paid double if one turned up in a presentable evening dress'). Shortly after drifting back to Watermead, she had succeeded in getting herself taken on as a part-time assistant to Mr Tripp, who managed the NAAFI canteen recently installed at the British Legion Hall in the village High Street; but this work was very poorly paid.

As Kay received no unearned income, she was always hard up. Her life was conditioned, and her movements restricted, by the nagging memory of innumerable small debts – many of them so minor that they had long ago been uncomplainingly written off by her creditors. But Kay's conventional upbringing, combined with her spontaneously generous nature, had made her essentially scrupulous over money matters, and the knowledge that she owed anything to anybody caused her genuine distress. She was equally punctilious about fulfilling the obligations imposed by formal 'good manners': if one gave Kay lunch, and then met her in the village before she had posted her letter of thanks, she would either try to avoid one altogether or would anticipate any greeting by a remorseful cry of 'I owe you a letter!' She was even more furtive if confronted unexpectedly by an acquaintance who had once lent her sixpence to tip a porter, or placed a modest bet for her on a losing horse in a long-past race because she had feared no bookie would give her credit.

Kay suffered from a congenital lack of energy, and after taking books out of W. H. Smith's lending libraries in Swindon or Marlborough she would succumb to a mysterious, destructive lassitude which prevented her from returning them until long after the dates written on the little tickets dangling reproachfully from their spines. Conscious of having incurred a debt which mounted terrifyingly with every day that went by, and unable to compute with even approximate accuracy the sum of the fines to which she might eventually be liable, she would postpone their settlement yet further. When at last Kay feared that some river of no return had been fatally crossed, she judged it too much of a risk to be seen passing W. H. Smith's shop windows in either town, and to escape notice, recognition and exposure she would condemn herself to inconvenient detours, dodging down side alleys or hiding behind traffic in the main streets except on safe Sundays and early-closing afternoons. Most of the borrowed books did in the end find their way back to the libraries (sometimes conveyed there by me) but one of her favourites – *Without My Cloak* by Kate O'Brien – still remained in her possession. Kay's sense of guilt at having in effect stolen *Without My Cloak* had become so overwhelming that she now refused to visit Marlborough or Swindon at all unless she was covered up in some sort of wrap as a token disguise – in fact (I made myself laugh at the thought as I waited for the hours to pass in my lonely dark hilltop watch) in those places she was *never* without her cloak!

At two o'clock in the morning I re-entered the hut. Harry was sleeping so deeply that his face no longer resembled a sentient countenance and the prominent Adam's apple in his long white neck, more than usually exposed by his supine position, seemed to be the most expressive feature in his body. I thought it might be difficult to wake him, but after a tentative touch on the shoulder his eyes opened at once and he submissively rose

41

from his bed. I lay down on mine but still could not sleep although my thoughts were becoming as painfully pictorial and uncontrollably inconsequent as dreams. They circled round a scene that had recently taken place at Watermead and which had been described to me in hallucinatory detail by Kay.

Father, mother and daughter were assembled in the sitting-room to listen to the BBC evening news. This programme was invariably preceded by a performance of the national anthem. On the night in question, as its opening chords were struck, an event took place at the Demarests' hearth that had never happened there before: apparently in hypnotized obedience to a sudden over-mastering impulse, Sybil had slowly and gracefully risen to her feet and had continued to stand stiffly to attention on the Axminster carpet, her blue eyes staring steadily ahead of her at the Ladbroke calendar on the mantelpiece in a solemn gaze which implied a combination of personal humility and patriotic pride.

Kay glanced up at her in bewilderment and then tactfully looked away. 'I thought Mummy was making a complete ass of herself by getting up on her hind legs like that but it's her own drawing-room and how she behaves in it is no business of anybody else's. Though I did find it devilishly embarrassing. To tell you the truth, I nearly went through the floor!'

A second or so later, Charlie noticed the alteration in his wife's posture, and he too eyed her in startled irritation for a moment before taking in the significance of her action. 'He's deaf as a post, you know, so he probably didn't even realize it was "God Save the King" they were playing. But when the penny finally dropped, of course *he* had to get in on the act as well!' Clumsily and apologetically, he clambered out of his armchair and stood frozen in a military stance even more rigid than his wife's, but with a look of fury on his face that contrasted comically with her expression of noble serenity.

Kay soon saw that Charlie's anger was directed at herself, and understood that he was silently accusing her of disloyalty to her country and irreverence to her God by continuing to remain seated in this exalted atmosphere. He made her feel, in fact, that she was doing nothing so innocent as merely sitting down, but that she was provocatively lolling, impertinently lounging, almost indecently sprawling. Part of her longed to get up ('Anything for a quiet life'), however ridiculous she would have considered such a surrender to the hypocritical hysteria that seemed to have seized her parents; but a greater part was gripped by the same moral paralysis and morbid passivity that prevented her from returning her library books on time, and she found to her horror that she was quite unable to move.

The spectacle of her stubborn stillness – which he interpreted as a wilful refusal to surmount a sickly, self-indulgent languor – drove Charlie to a climax of exasperation where he lost all control. Grunting inaudible curses, he abandoned the pretence of respect due to the anthem which was still playing on the radio and precipitately stumbled to a point just behind Kay's armchair. He then began to push vigorously against its back in a frenzied attempt to overturn it, with the intention of tipping her on to the carpet. But the solid weight of the chair frustrated this plan, and all he managed to do was to shove it forward a few inches, still bearing the inert figure of his daughter, who was now seriously frightened.

The music stopped and Sybil, who had pointedly ignored Charlie's slapstick antics by preserving a sentry-like immobility during the whole episode, felt free to relax at last; raising her dress a little over her hips so as not to 'seat out' her skirt, she gravely lowered herself back into her chair. Charlie returned to his and the three of them proceeded to listen to the news, cosily grouped round the wireless like so many other anxious families throughout the beleaguered country, the only evidence of anything

43

untoward having occurred being the sound of Charlie's panting and the fact that Kay's chair had been shifted slightly askew from its accustomed position.

The vivacity with which Kay recounted such secret family dramas made her an amusing companion on a walk, or indoors by the gramophone, gossiping while she painted her nails a new colour after we had read our daily horoscopes (and those of absent friends) or competed in a private game which consisted of naming as many of Carole Lombard's films as we could remember. But I knew that the hostility she inspired in her parents hurt her like a constantly throbbing wound, and as I lay in the hut on the desolate aerodrome I longed to help her to escape from their petty persecution and give the wound a chance to heal.

The sun rose during my second watch. The gardens behind the houses on the southern side of the High Street, which enviably bordered on the river, became visible in detail as the light gained strength. From some of these I had been allowed to bathe as a child. An early ray caught the glass conservatory at the back of the doctor's surgery, transforming it into a brilliant translucent globe which seemed on the point of floating free from the building to which it was attached. Some elemental quality about its bulbous shape and crystalline consistency must have corresponded to an obscure stimulus in my pre-conscious memory, for the sight had the same unsettling effect on me – an acute aesthetic nostalgia – as that of the pointed white tents, glimpsed from a distance through the window of a moving car, which used to materialize on Salisbury Plain during peacetime army manoeuvres.

Above the High Street, I could see the churchyard where my father had been buried at the beginning of the year, and just beyond it the other garden, which did not yet show any palpable signs of decay as a result of his inability to tend it. And above the other garden, my home. For some reason, the curtains of my bedroom window had been drawn the night before: I confusedly imagined that behind them I must be still asleep in bed. My long vigil had left me shrouded in a fierce fatigue, an insubstantial but poisonous vapour which seemed to spread back into my past and seep ahead into my future, staining not only my body and mind but also my entire existence. Through it, I was dimly aware that rest and relief were near. Soon I would stagger down the hill with Harry Vokins and, after parting with him at the paper shop, would walk up through the churchyard in a dream, my steps growing heavier and heavier as they approached the house. This would appear oddly unfamiliar, as the impression made by a place seen for the first time differs subtly from the way in which it is later known and remembered. Once back upstairs in my own bed – and for as long as I remained there – I would be safe: safe from the war with its teasing threat of further death and its yet more fearsome challenge to an intenser form of life than any I had known.

IV

When I reached Oxford I discovered Billy Phipps already in residence at the same college. It soon became clear that our former friendship had lost its point although at first we made half-hearted attempts to keep it going. He invited me to come out beagling with him and announced that he had put me up for membership of the Gridiron, one of several clubs to which he belonged. I ignored the first suggestion and, since I heard no more of the second, could only assume that I had been embarrassingly blackballed by Billy's fellow members.

His wizened worldliness no longer struck me as a respectable form of sophistication, although this quality still seemed desirable in my eyes – partly because I didn't understand its precise meaning and so could never be sure if I had correctly diagnosed its presence or not. I was persuaded that it was less likely to be found among the undergraduates at the depleted University of those war years than in the busy town, which then housed the personnel of various Government Ministries evacuated from London. The friends I finally made were mainly art students at the Slade School, which had also moved from bomb-threatened Bloomsbury to premises in Oxford. The most gifted of these, the most flamboyant and the most delightful, was Denis Bellamy, whom I got to know during my second term.

Being with Denis was like finding oneself in the cast of an 'intimate revue' or a lavish Hollywood musical, unprepared for the performance but secure because the star would carry one. He spoke with the dizzily inventive timing of a comedian and moved with the lazy discipline of a dancer. One might be walking with him from his rooms in Walton Street to the Randolph bar, discussing Géricault's studies of the insane or Blake's engravings, when he would suddenly break into a rumba in the middle of Beaumont Street, singing in imitation of Hermione Gingold: 'And when I'm *out* with *Jack* I really *find* the *black*-out very pleasant ... 'cos his moustache is phos*phoresc*ent!' – his voice rising to a wild shriek on the last word; or else impulsively dash up the steps of the Ashmolean and then descend them at a stately pace with his body turned a little to one side, his arms extended in a graceful pose and a condescending smile of ecstatic self-admiration on his lips, pretending to be Hedy Lamarr or Lana Turner in the 'You Stepped Out of a Dream' number from *Ziegfeld Girl*, while he crooned an improvised parody of the lyric: '*You* stepped out of a *drain* ... Where did you *get* that hat? ... You look quite *insane* ...'

He was tall and thin, with thick chestnut hair, high cheekbones and large eyes and mouth; although he dressed conventionally, some inner lack of inhibition must have shown through the grey flannel trousers and tweed jackets because people often stared at him with disapproval in the street and – by the rigid standards governing masculine comportment at the time – he was considered somewhat outrageous. But Denis was without any exhibitionist desire to shock and his charm was entirely unaffected. He conformed naturally to some aspects of the current 'camp' culture but his wit was never bitchy and his character had no trace of competitive envy. Somewhere in his make-up was a down-to-earth, no-nonsense North Country landlady who would give sound practical advice when consulted and had no time to waste on any form of pretentiousness. In love he was ardent and artless, either romantically faithful while an important affair lasted or dangerously promiscuous after it had come to grief. As a friend he was loyal and generous: when one of his paintings was included in a mixed show at the Leicester Galleries in London and subsequently sold, he gave all the proceeds to a girl student at the Slade who needed money for an abortion. He had been tubercular for years but quixotically refused to seek treatment for the disease or to follow the careful régime that might prevent it from getting worse.

I did not see as much of Denis as I would have wished during that spring and summer – he was not only in great demand from other friends but also absorbed both in his work at the Slade, where he was a brilliantly promising pupil, and in the cliff-hanging serial of his erotic adventures – but I found that even a short time in his company would cheer me up to such an extent that I did not grudge his absences. In between our meetings, I mooched about Oxford, haunted by the hit song – 'Blues in the Night' – which floated ceaselessly through open windows in the town and from distant river-boats. The music uncannily epitomized a tempting mood of solitary sadness, unfocused longing and vague expectation into which it was all too easy to sink.

Shortly after his twenty-first birthday party (which started with drinks at the Playhouse bar, moved on to the George for dinner and ended with an all-night dance at a don's house in Holywell) Denis had a serious haemorrhage. This frightened him into taking the advice which his friends had been proffering for so long: he went into hospital at last. He wrote me a letter from a sanatorium in Cornwall. 'There's a funny idea going around that consumption is romantic – you know, Mimi or *La Dame aux Camélias* daintily coughing blood into a lace hankie and Katherine Mansfield drawing her *chaise-longue* a little bit closer to the window every day. Well, my dear, don't you believe a word of it! TB couldn't be more squalid if it tried – take it from Mother, she knows! They're going to collapse one of my lungs, which I'm told is "unpleasant" but not the worst. What I'm terrified of is having to have some of my ribs removed, but with luck that won't be necessary. I've got a mania for Elizabeth Bowen and am reading all her books. I'm dying to know what she's like. There's a very arty lady here with her hair done in "earphones" – exactly like Gingold in that sketch where she gives a lecture on "mew-sick". Well, the doctor told her the other day that she hasn't much longer to live. It's rather got me down because she's really awfully sweet ... Among all the patients there's only one who's rather attractive, but he's almost cured and is probably leaving next month. Another myth about this illness is that it makes everybody madly randy. God, I hope I get out of here soon!'

After Denis's departure, the sense of unreality which I had felt at Oxford from the start grew more oppressive. It was June 1942, and I was nearing the end of my third term. The beauty of the place in summer only seemed to enhance its latent melancholy. I saw little point in working for a good degree when the future (my own, the world's) was so uncertain. In retreat from a looming depression, I tried to get back home as often as I could. There was no great distance between the University and my village, but a comfortable and reliable method of covering it was frustratingly hard to find. The two places were only indirectly linked by an inconvenient network of stopping trains with ill-timed connections and rare rural buses; petrol rationing had ensured a scarcity of private motorists; hitchhiking on lorries and trucks was a chancy business.

Kay Demarest, however, had worked out a scheme by which I might travel in security and for nothing. She was one of those people who enjoyed inventing ingenious ways round minor difficulties, whether these were imposed by the war or not; for example, rather than risk posting an expensive parcel to London, she would find out whether a friend of a friend might know somebody who was going there anyway, and would sometimes succeed in persuading a complete stranger to act as her courier. The more complicated the plan, the greater would be her gratification at its execution. She now suggested that I should be given a lift in the car which delivered cake to the NAAFI where she worked; she had discovered that it began its rounds at Oxford. After lengthy preparations, she wrote to tell me that it was all fixed: I could 'come with the cake'.

Kay arranged a rendezvous for me and my transport at seven o'clock one Saturday morning outside the entrance to the Cadena Café in the Cornmarket. I had been waiting there for half an hour before a small van drew up driven by a woman dressed rather like a Land Girl: she told me to hop into the seat beside her. Behind us, a pile of cardboard cartons and tin boxes rattled when we moved. These contained various kinds of cake: small hard rock scones, fat Swiss rolls, truncated segments of dark Dundee and pale Madeira in transparent wrappings and samples of fancier brands such as marzipan layer and lemon curd sandwich confined in coffin-shaped cases.

The journey turned out to be the longest and most boring that I had ever undertaken. The van slowly traversed a meandering cross-country route linking hamlet to village to market town, in each of which one or more leisurely deliveries were made at British Restaurants or NAAFI and Church Army canteens housed in municipal buildings or newly erected Nissen huts, as well as at several commercial cafés and one isolated farm house in the middle of open fields. The driver never spoke, and neither did I: perhaps we both didn't like to be the first to do so. It was nearly seven in the evening when, stiff and weary and hungry, I was deposited at our destination in the High Street of my own village – only a distance of about thirty miles as a crow might have flown from the spot where we started out.

This sluggish pilgrimage reminded me of my night on

Home Guard duty the previous year and, as then, I spent some of the time thinking about Kay, whom I expected to find waiting to greet me when it was over. My mother had recently passed on to me some dramatic news concerning the Demarests. A month or so earlier, Sandy's plane had been shot down over occupied France and he had been reported missing, believed killed. But only a few days later, his family were officially informed that he had been captured alive and unhurt by German forces, and was now a prisoner of war. Knowing Kay's instinctive preference for undemonstrative behaviour, I decided not to mention this subject unless she did.

She didn't; but the relief she must still have been feeling after hearing of Sandy's reprieve was shown in the elation of her welcome. 'How wonderful! You made it!' she exclaimed, while the driver was helping the canteen manager to unload his order from the back of her van. 'You actually came with the cake! I'm so glad it worked out all right – you must often do it again. Listen, Mr Tripp has given me the evening off, so now that you're here let's go on a pub crawl. I need cheering up. This morning I heard some rather touching news. My friend Roy Halma wrote to tell me that poor Ernest has died. He's frightfully cut up about it ... But you must be starving. Here, have a slice of this coffee gâteau before we set out. It's on the house!'

Owing to the scarcity of spirits, cigarettes and even matches, a pub crawl in those days took on something of the glamour of a quest. There were seven to choose from in the village, ranging from the stately Lion in the centre of the High Street, which was also a small hotel, to a minute, nameless back-room in a Beatrix Potter cottage standing by itself at the far end of a lonely lane. Word would get round that one or other of these had received a consignment of Gordon's or Player's Weights – but when one got there, more often than not, it was to find that the gin had run out already and rum was on offer instead, while the cigarettes were only being sold singly or in pairs, carelessly handed over the bar in a sodden, stained condition and smelling of stale beer.

Kay and I fetched up in the back-room of the cottage, rather drunk on several pints of bitter and a few glasses of sweet, sticky rum. We each had one Weight left, but nothing with which to light them.

'Leave it to me,' said Kay. She boldly surveyed the small, almost empty room. A GI was standing on his own at the bar. 'Just watch this,' she murmured, and with her 'tarty' walk she approached and (there is no other word) accosted him.

'Got a match, soldier?' she asked, flourishing her damp, discoloured gasper as stylishly as if it had been a Balkan Sobranie in an ivory holder. The GI produced a lighter and as she ducked her head to the flame he said, 'Did anyone ever tell you that you looked like Jean Harlow?'

Kay lifted her head and fixed her eyes on his in an expressionless stare while she slowly dragged on her cigarette and, after an alarmingly long pause, exhaled the smoke through her nose. 'What's it to you if they have? Mind your own business!' she said rudely, and then rather grudgingly added, 'Oh – and thanks for the fire.' She sauntered back to her former place, where she lit my cigarette from hers.

She was obviously very pleased with this exchange. 'Funny he should say that,' she mused. 'Nobody's ever told me that before, as it happens. People used to say I looked like Joan Crawford. But that was ages ago, when she first started. Speaking for myself, I shouldn't have thought I was the Harlow type at all – can't see the faintest resemblance, frankly. I can *just* see Crawford, but for the life of me I can't see Harlow.'

There was in fact no physical resemblance between Kay and either of these actresses, but it struck me then that her manner with men in a potentially sexual context must have been strongly influenced by that of Joan Crawford on the screen. This manner would swing between two extremes. At one, the woman in the film who suspected some guy of 'getting fresh' with her would be bad-tempered, impatient, quite unnecessarily snubbing and sometimes almost unforgivably insulting. Watching some of Joan Crawford's performances, I had been reminded of the way a bitch on heat behaves to a dog who is sniffing her hindquarters – venomously snapping at him and leaping away as if in furious outrage, but somehow still remaining on hand. At the other extreme, reached with apparently arbitrary abruptness and with no intervening gradations of mood, she would melt into a state of exalted tenderness and submissiveness so totally overwhelming as to produce a stifling effect of menace ... Kay's favourite films – *Man's Castle* and *Strange Cargo* – were romantic melodramas, and she often affected an air of sentimental toughness which made me think of Joan Crawford and other movie stars who played hard-working, hard-done-by women ready and able to humiliate the harmless men they despise but also – and not always convincingly – capable of suicidal sacrifice for the cruel men they love. It was the sentimental toughness of numerous popular songs between the wars, celebrating the sordid lives of tired taxi-dancers, heartbroken tarts and ill-used one-man-girls which managed to distil a heady drop of bittersweet poetry from trite and depressing themes.

Shortly before closing time, I had to go to the pub's primitive Gents. While I was pissing against a wall in the yard, I became aware of the GI doing the same beside me. 'Is she on the make?' he suddenly asked.

I was embarrassed and pretended not to understand him.

'The dame you're with – is she on the make?' he patiently repeated. I could think of nothing better to reply than, 'I don't know.'

The three of us left the pub together. The GI was called Howard Spangler – a quiet, courteous young man, short and thickset with a large, low bottom. I left them outside the Lion, taking the path home through the churchyard while they walked slowly on down the High Street. The GI was whistling the tune of 'Stardust' and Kay was singing the words.

When I next saw Kay, she told me that she had fallen in love with Howard Spangler and was having an affair with him.

'Did you go to bed with him that night after the pub?' I asked.

'Well, not exactly – but as near as makes no matter! I went to field with him, if you really want to know!'

Kay's graphic answer brought home to me for the first time the inadequacy of the current euphemism for lovemaking which I had used as a matter of course, and initiated another of our private jokes. On a later occasion, Kay announced that she had 'gone to floor' with Howard Spangler – the floor being that of the NAAFI canteen. 'And damned hard it was, too!'

The joke, however, was a wry one, underlining the fact that Kay had no place of her own where she could meet her lover in comfort. (To present him to her parents was out of the question: an earlier wartime romance of Kay's, with a Captain in an infantry regiment stationed near Swindon, had fizzled out because Charlie had banned him from Watermead on the grounds that 'he couldn't speak the King's English'.) At first, the pride and fun in 'having an American' raised Kay's spirits to a point where she could laugh about this handicap, and even find in it a welcome element of melodrama to dignify the rather prosaic relationship that had developed between Howard and herself. But, almost from the beginning, she feared that it could not last. Other GIs who had taken up with women in the village were enjoying fringe benefits in addition to simple sexual satisfaction: home cooking, cosy domestic interiors, a friendly social atmosphere, and it was mainly for these that they paid happily with gifts of chewing gum, peanut butter and Lucky Strikes. Apart from her own body, and a provocative line in movie-script repartee, poor Kay had only the fields and the NAAFI floor to offer Howard, and she doubted that this would be enough to hold him for long.

My mother assured Kay that she and Howard could meet at our house whenever they liked, but this did not solve her problem: army officers had been billeted on us, occupying more than half the available space, and the part retained for our own use was too exiguous to accommodate a lovers' tryst. Kay did, however, arrange for Howard to pick her up at our place on one of their dates. She was anxious to introduce him to my mother – hoping thus to sketch in, as it were, some sort of respectable background for herself.

Kay turned up hours before Howard was due to arrive, wearing her familiar uniform of headscarf, slacks and shoulder-bag – the latter unusually heavy, as in addition to its regular load of knitting, cigarettes and magazines it also contained various cosmetic preparations (mascara, nail polish, Odorono) as well as a change of costume. Clothes of course were rationed then, and women used to buy, borrow or swap each others' garments. Kay had been lent a skirt by Mrs Tripp, the wife of her boss at the NAAFI, and my mother gave her one of her own blouses to go with it. Kay had also brought with her a bottle of some liquid application with which to stain her naked legs and produce the illusion that she was wearing nylon stockings. Howard was expected to call for her at seven; he had promised to escort her to a dance at the Village Hall, in aid of the local Women's Institute, and had been invited to 'look in' for a drink with us first.

But he didn't show up at seven. By nine o'clock, Kay conceded that he was unlikely to do so that evening. She had been looking forward so intensely to the outing that we expected her disappointment to be devastating. Kay surprised us by appearing neither hurt nor angry but, if anything, rather relieved. 'Well, at least I can relax now in something comfortable!' she said, as she changed back into her everyday attire and wiped the make-up off her face. 'I do think he might have let us know – but it's probably not his fault. One does tend to forget that these people are fighting a war.'

'What a shame,' said my mother. 'I would so much like to have met him.'

'I think you'd have got on with him if you had. Mind you, he's no oil painting, that I grant. And he's not exactly what one's parents would call a gentleman – ghastly expression – but we're none of us snobs here, are we? Oh, to hell with him. I'm going to celebrate by making myself look as ugly as possible! To which no doubt you might say: *that* wouldn't be hard!'

For years Kay had suffered from a dread of looking her best when there was nobody to admire the effect she made, of being 'all dressed up with nowhere to go.' She was the opposite of those legendary imperialists who insisted on changing for dinner in the jungle. The wasted effort involved in such disciplined behaviour did not just strike her as comically pointless – its crazy conventionality contained for her a peculiar element of horror. The experience of being stood up by Howard Spangler promoted this characteristic of hers from a mild neurosis to a morbid obsession.

Kay never again applied make-up to her face and body or put on a pretty garment: she seemed to take a grim delight in 'letting her looks go' altogether. This extreme reaction was probably prompted by a romantic pride, with perhaps a touch of conceit. Kay longed for a lover, longed for a husband, longed for children – but she was only interested in the kind of man who would 'take her as she was', independent of any artificial aids to beauty or simulated allure. Did she see herself as a sleeping Brünhilde, preserved by a ring of fire from any but the most heroic suitor? I think her attitude was less arrogant – she merely wanted to spare herself the hideous humiliation of trying

56

to attract, and failing.

So instead she gave the false impression of trying to repel. Kay stalked the streets and lanes, still (as it seemed to me) an arresting and pleasing figure, but so gaunt in outline, so bereft of the accepted manifestations of feminine charm, that she almost seemed a creature for whom definition by age or sex would have hardly any meaning. Some of her back teeth had recently had to be drawn and she resolutely and perversely refused to have them replaced by false ones, thus giving her face an unnecessarily sunken, even a skeletal appearance. Kay's stated reason for this deliberate neglect was an understandable reluctance to incur large dentist's bills, but I think she was really motivated by the irrational valour of the stoic for whom self-mutilation may be a secret challenge to the inevitability of decay, a device to negate its terrors by hastening its approach.

Howard was soon scared off: shortly after the broken date he vanished from her life. I once overheard her discussed by two other American soldiers outside the Lion – they said she looked like the witch in *Snow White*. There was nothing witch-like (either black or white) in the Kay I knew and loved; rather, she seemed to me the hapless victim of a mysterious spell binding her to the callous custody of her parents.

No doubt because her waking life was so unsatisfactory, Kay paid close attention to her dreams. Some passing reference of mine, during one of our long walks by the river, would cause her to exclaim, 'You've broken my dream!' – and she would then describe it to me in detail. Often her very first remark, when we met by arrangement at the paper shop before the walk, would be, 'I dreamed about you last night.' The news that I had featured in Kay's dreams was flattering, even exciting, but also rather disturbing, and my instinct on hearing it would be to apologize for any crass, boorish or unseemly behaviour of which I might have been unconsciously guilty: it was hard not to feel that the responsibility for my speech and actions in her dream was mine instead of hers. But it always turned out that I had played a harmless, and usually a subsidiary, role: the star part, more often than not, belonged to Sandy. Night after night, Kay would dream that she was with him somewhere in Europe; blissfully happy, she would be sitting by a trout stream while in companionable silence he squatted on the bank beside her intently choosing a fly from his colourful collection of purples and browns, or stood tall in the water laying his line across the ripples with a kind of hesitant courtesy, as though diffidently but gracefully executing a respectful bow. Screened by trees on the opposite shore, she could dimly see the prison camp from which he had either escaped, or been let out on forty-eight hours' leave: in obedience to the scrambled logic of dreams, it looked exactly like Watermead.

V

Later that summer, I was invited to a tea party by Dodo at Love's Cottage, where she now lived all the year round; Charlie and Sybil were to be the other guests. I arrived early to find Dodo chortling to herself over *What I Left Unsaid*, a book of memoirs by an old friend of hers, Daisy, Princess of Pless. 'Oh, dear, she *could* be such a silly ass! Just listen to this – it's the first sentence of her chapter on King Edward's Coronation: "London was upside down – and so was Daisy!" That *might* have been phrased a tiny bit more elegantly, don't you agree? As one of the reviewers remarked – it would have been better if she *had* left it unsaid!'

I asked her if the Demarests had had any news of Sandy and she told me that letters from him had indeed reached Watermead, that he was in good health and spirits, well enough treated by his captors and complaining only of boredom. 'It is such a pity', Dodo went on, 'that Kay and her parents can't get on a bit better: it would worry Sandy so terribly if he knew. I must say, brother and sister aren't at all alike – she's a striking girl in many ways but she certainly doesn't have Sandy's looks. I believe there *was* some gossip – but I'm sure it was nonsense – that after Kay turned out to be a girl Sybil changed the bowling.'

'You mean, that Charlie isn't Sandy's real father?'

'But I don't believe it for one instant. One could understand a woman doing that when the family were longing for a son and there'd only been rows of daughters, but in this case it really would have been a little soon – and it's not as if an old title were involved, or a big place somewhere, or anything like that. Help! – here they come, I can see them through the window. Wouldn't it be awful if they knew what we'd just been saying about them?'

Sybil entered the cottage carrying several copies of a new novel by John Steinbeck called *The Moon Is Down*: she pressed one of these on me and one on Dodo. 'I simply insist on you both reading this book at the very earliest opportunity you get. I came across it quite by chance – a friend lent it to me, as a matter of fact – and it impressed me so deeply that as soon as I had finished it I wrote off at once to Hatchards and ordered two dozen copies. I make a point of giving it to everyone I meet – well, everyone, that is, whom I consider capable of appreciating it. I won't say anything about what it's about, for fear of spoiling your pleasure, but if you're anything like me you won't be able to put it down. Charlie will tell you that it's very rare for me to go off the deep end about a thing like this, won't you, Charlie?'

'Certainly,' said Charlie. 'The last time she had a craze was for that weird musical play, *The Immortal Hour*. I think she went forty times!'

'Oh, wasn't it divine?' said Dodo. 'That heavenly song – "How beautiful they are, the lordly ones, who dwell in the hills, the hollow hills ..." Oh dear, my voice has quite gone, but I think that's roughly how it went. I always thought "the lordly ones" was rather a ridiculous phrase, to tell you the truth, but it's such a pretty melody. How sweet of you to give me this book, darling, it looks lovely.'

'I found it most inspiring. I should perhaps warn you that it's not for the squeamish – but for Heaven's sake don't run away with the idea that it's in any way offensive! I only mean that it doesn't come under the heading of what is now called "escapist" entertainment. On the other hand, there is absolutely nothing defeatist about it. If there's one thing that makes me see red, it's defeatism. Oh dear, there are moments when I do so desperately wish I'd been born a man! Don't you?'

Dodo had quietly left the room to fetch a milk jug from the kitchen, so Sybil found that she had addressed these last words to Charlie and myself.

'Oh – but of course you *are* men! Needless to say, I never for one second intended to imply anything to the contrary and did not expect to be taken *au pied de la lettre*. No, the point I was trying to make is that, *being* men, you couldn't possibly either of you hope to enter into a woman's feelings about certain subjects.' She raised her voice. 'Dodo, dear! I was just saying how much I wished I were a man. Don't you?'

'Do you mean, do I wish you were a man, or do I wish I was?' said Dodo, rejoining us. 'On the whole, I think I'm all right as I am. I mean, one has the vote. I know one ought to be frightfully grateful to the suffragettes for fighting our battles for us, but I'm afraid I did think them an awful nuisance at the time.'

Charlie muttered something about race meetings having to be cancelled.

'No, dear,' said Sybil, 'you don't quite understand me ... It's just that I sometimes find myself envying the male sex its God-given right to quite simply go out there and take a jolly good swipe at the enemy. Not that I'm the slightest bit bloodthirsty by nature. I'm quite prepared to carry on doing my bit by just carrying on – which is what we poor women are always being asked to do – but I do on occasion feel an overwhelming urge to *get cracking*! Don't you?'

'I sometimes think if I'm told one more time to carry on,' said Dodo naughtily, 'I *shall*!'

'I do believe', Sybil continued, 'that when the history books come to be written it will emerge that the great unsung heroine of these terrible times we're living through will be none other than that much maligned creature, the British Housewife! I'm thinking, in fact, of writing a letter to the *Daily Telegraph* to propose that some promising young sculptor – or perhaps a *sculptress* would be a better choice – should be officially commissioned to design a statue in her honour, and that the result should be prominently erected in some public place. I don't know about you, but I for one am getting sick and tired of looking at monuments portraying middle-aged men on horseback!'

'Where's the money going to come from?' asked Charlie. 'Out of the taxpayer's pocket, you can bet your boots, as per usual.'

'I'm terribly sorry, but I had rather imagined – naively, no doubt – that the artist and stonemasons concerned on such a project might be willing to work for nothing. However, if sufficient funds are not forthcoming,' Sybil went on, 'perhaps it might be humbly suggested to His Majesty King George VI that a brand new medal might be struck, to be awarded at the appropriate times of the year to a selection of especially deserving women who would stand as representatives of each and every British Housewife in the land. But, very likely, reasons will be found to prove this scheme impractical, too – I confess to being an incorrigible idealist! Though I can't help thinking it would do a power of good as regards the not un-negligible matter of boosting the nation's morale.'

'You mentioned the King,' said Dodo. 'Well, personally, I think it would give a boost to the nation's morale if the female members of the Royal Family had a tiny bit more dress sense! You never saw such an un-clothes-conscious bunch! Queen Elizabeth's fur-trimmed coats are becoming almost as tiresome as old Queen Mary's *toques*!' (Dodo pronounced the last word with a French accent, and I did not immediately recognize it.) 'The only one with any claim to *chic* was dear Queen Alexandra. Her taste was always flawless.'

'But I shall never forgive her – never,' said Sybil, 'for going into colours so soon after King Edward's death. I think in that respect she showed far from flawless taste. In fact, I think she showed deplorable lack of respect and quite indecent haste! I can't remember precisely how long she waited, but it seemed that in no time at all she was appearing before the public – not in *demi-deuil*, nothing like that – but in the brightest hues of the rainbow! I'm afraid it set a very poor example to the rest of us.'

'Oh, I think those long periods of public mourning were such a dreary hypocritical Victorian custom!' said Dodo. 'I was only too thankful to see them begin to go out of fashion after what I always call *our* war – and if they're completely done away with after this one, then that would be *one* good thing to come out of it, at least.'

'I feel very differently,' said Sybil, 'but it's a tricky question and we really *shouldn't* quarrel over it so shall we just agree to differ? To change the subject, I must say I do think you're not *quite* fair to the Royals. You're forgetting the Duchess of Kent.'

'Oh yes, so I am. She's too lovely, isn't she? *And* she dresses divinely. How silly of me – she completely slipped my mind.'

'Princess Marina', said Sybil, 'not only dresses divinely, as you say, but with what I can only describe as that elusive thing called "style". To illustrate my point one need look no further than her sister-in-law, Wallis Warfield Simpson. (I'm sorry, but I flatly refuse to refer to her by her courtesy title!) Wallis Warfield Simpson proves that it is perfectly possible to spend a great deal of money on smart clothes and still look rather common. You see, it all boils down to breeding in the end, like so much else. Take good looks, for example. So many of these pretty little faces that people make such a fuss about nowadays – these pin-up girls and blonde bombshells and so on and so forth – won't last *five minutes* over the age of, say, twenty-five.'

'What the French call *la beauté du diable*,' said Dodo.

'But Princess Marina has bone structure. That's what counts. She happens to be still a young woman but her age is neither here nor there. With bone structure like that one could easily be a raving beauty at the age of ninety.'

'It's absolutely true,' said Dodo wistfully. 'I never had it myself, so I know! Without bone structure, one's too fearfully *journalière* – looking one's very best on a good evening and then, for no known reason, like the back of a bus the next day!'

'I agree with Sybil,' said Charlie. 'There's a darn sight too much emphasis placed on youth nowadays by people old enough to know better. It's all a lot of rot – you're as old as you feel, always have been.'

'But that's just the trouble!' said Dodo. 'I feel a hundred! If I'd *only* had the courage – not to mention the cash – to get a face-lift when the time was ripe, I'm quite sure it would have done me the world of good. But I didn't quite dare and now, alas, I've left it too late.'

Charlie chuckled. 'That reminds me of rather a nice story a friend of mine tells. You probably know it – the one about the ageing film star who went and had her face lifted. Only trouble was – it fell again when she got the bill!'

The tepid laughter which greeted Charlie's joke was broken into by Sybil.

'But, Dodo *darling*,' she protested, 'you will persist in the fallacy that good looks are everything! It's just too silly of you for words! I'm quite cross with you – you ought to know better! Now you just listen to me. If a young woman who felt that she was hanging fire came to me for advice, I would tell her exactly what my own mother told me when I first came out. "Never, never be a bore! It is the unpardonable sin! Men don't give a damn about anything else but they *cannot* stand being bored! When you're put next to somebody at a dinner party, for Heaven's sake, *say* something. It scarcely matters what – the first thing that enters your head will be better than nothing – just so long as you don't sit there in dead silence like a stuffed dummy while *he*, poor fellow, has to rack his brains in search of some polite way of opening the conversation. You may be looking as pretty as a picture – it makes no earthly difference. Never, never", my mother would say, "underrate the value of small talk. It is vital to be well-informed – though don't, whatever you do, let him think that you're too brainy, because that can be fatal as well. But somehow or other find the time to read *all* the morning papers from cover to cover, so that you have some idea of what is going on in the rest of the world and need not be at a loss for a suitable topic. You'll find that men will put up with a lot, but they will run a *mile* from a woman who bores them, even if she is as lovely to look upon as Helen of Troy." And that advice of my mother's has stood me in very good stead. Not, let me hasten to add, that I am in the slightest bit intolerant of bores *myself*. In fact, I really don't believe that I would recognize a bore if I came face to face with one. You see, I'm lucky – I am never bored! I'm desperately sorry for my friends when they complain of boredom, but the truth is that I don't know what the heck they're talking about! There always – in whatever situation I happen to find myself – seems to be something to occupy my mind – to interest or amuse me. Sad, yes – deeply moved – frustrated – angry – hurt – all these on occasion I may be. But bored – never. I don't know the meaning of the word!'

Sybil triumphantly surveyed her audience. Charlie and I were staring at our shoes, and Dodo had fallen asleep.

After tea, as I walked through the other garden back to the house, I recalled what Kay had said when she heard that I was going to see her parents again. 'Remember, they're on their best behaviour when you meet them socially. They can be perfectly charming if they care to try. But they're hell to live with. And she's far the worst. He's all right on his own, so long as one keeps out of his way. But she seems to set out deliberately in search of some fault she can find with me. And if she fails to find it, she'll invent one. I don't know why she hates me so much. I'm not aware of having done her any harm. She always gets her own way with Daddy and Sandy – I'm no threat to her there. An ex-boyfriend of mine who's a bit of a highbrow – you know the type, lives in Bloomsbury and writes books – he said it was Freudian. Said she was in love with Sandy and jealous of me because I was younger than her. But I think that's too far-fetched. It's true that, when I first grew up, one of her admirers seemed to fancy me and there was the most God-almighty dust-up. But nothing of that kind has happened since. No, I think she's just never liked me, from the moment I was born. Perhaps she had a particularly bad delivery, or something. I suppose it's not really her fault. It must be awful to have a child and just not like it. Almost as bad as being the child.'

There seemed to be no way of freeing Kay from her parents (and, for that matter, ridding them of her), although my mother and I tried again and again to think of one. However, early the following year, an opportunity presented itself for her at least to achieve a comparative independence by earning more money than her present tiny salary. A team of smartly uniformed American Red Cross workers had arrived in the neighbourhood and were busy establishing a canteen at the aerodrome. This was to be an elaborate and glamorous affair, as superior to the High Street NAAFI as the Ritz Hotel to an ABC, and the organizers had advertised for auxiliary helpers among the local ladies. It was rumoured that there were a great many vacancies and that the jobs would be extremely well paid. Kay applied for an interview, and was told to appear at eleven sharp one morning outside the Lion, where a jeep would be ready to drive her and a few other applicants to the Red Cross headquarters on the hill.

Shortly after eleven on the day of the interview I saw the forlorn figure of Kay turn into the drive of our house and struggle through the piercing cold and squally wind of a February sleet-storm to the front door. She almost collapsed when I let her in. She had been a few minutes late for the appointment and the jeep had left without her; she couldn't possibly walk up the hill in this weather; she had missed her chance of the job.

'It's so humiliating – something like this always happens – what *is* it about me? First one thing cropped up to detain me, then another, it seemed I just *couldn't* make a start ... And when I finally did get off, I had to run all the way so I arrived sweating and breathless and exhausted and feeling quite mad ... Why couldn't the bloody car have waited a few seconds longer? I was *so* nearly on time ... But it's obviously hopeless, I'll never be able to manage to get through life like other people do, I can't seem to cope with even the simplest challenge, it's no good my trying any longer, whatever I do is doomed to go wrong ...'

Kay stopped speaking and broke down in agonized tears. It was the first time I had seen her lose control in this way and I was completely unnerved by the experience. I felt confronted by something unspeakably piteous, as if forced to witness a scene of physical torture or hearing from a soul in hell, and yet Kay's words struck me as in no way out of the ordinary. The bleak message they conveyed gave a straightforward, balanced account of how the world can appear to people invisibly handicapped by a certain kind of temperament, and Kay's was an extreme example in which I recognized some elements of my own.

Once her crying fit was over, Kay acknowledged that her despair had been out of all proportion to its immediate cause; after several telephone calls, it was arranged for her to be included in a second batch of candidates later in the week. She felt that the interview had gone reasonably well, and when asked to undergo a routine medical examination she interpreted this development as a hopeful sign. But an X-ray of her chest revealed a dark patch on her left lung; further tests confirmed tuberculosis as the cause. Employment with the Red Cross was out of the question: she was urgently advised to see a specialist. After consultation with the Demarests' family doctor, she was sent off to the same Cornish sanatorium where Denis Bellamy had spent the last eight months.

I immediately wrote to Denis to tell him about Kay, and soon after her arrival there she wrote herself. '... I adore your friend Denis and feel he's already saved my life in this ghastly dump. He came bursting into my room on my first evening here, looking too extraordinary in a bright green silk night shirt, and said, "Now, dear, you've got to tell me all about the Bright Young Things in the Twenties!" I said, "That's going a bit far back, I'm afraid, but I'll tell you all about the Thirties with pleasure." He says he wants to paint me. There was an awful "atmosphere" before I left Watermead – Daddy livid because this place is so expensive, and Mummy saying, "It's all a lot of fuss about nothing if you ask me, nobody's ever been chesty on *my* side of the family, the best thing to do would be to hide the thermometer from Kay, she looks a very healthy invalid in my humble opinion!" Typical! Denis sends tons of love and so do I. Kay.'

VI

'Two letters for you – lucky man!' said Sister, holding them behind her back. 'I'll hand them over in a tick – but first I want to take a look at how you're getting on with my belt. My word, you *are* a slow coach! Better buck up about it, you know – I can't wait for ever!'

Sister's belt was a strip of leather on which I was clumsily stitching a childish pattern of bunny-rabbits, daisies, sunflowers and lambs in wools of varying pastel shades. I had already completed one belt of almost identical design for Sister, which she was wearing while she spoke, and I thought it rather odd of her to be so impatient for a second. The pointless labour on which I was employed was known in the convalescent home as occupational therapy. Sister had started me off with knitting, but I had made such a hash of this that I was soon encouraged to turn to crochet work, thought by her to be simpler: trimming leather belts had been the third and last resort.

The military convalescent home was situated in one wing of a large country house in East Anglia and the vast dormitory in which I lay had once been the ballroom. It was now bare of everything except for sixteen army beds arranged in two parallel rows: as in a barracks, the tops and bottoms of the beds were alternately reversed, so that the head of each occupant was on a level with the feet of his neighbours on either side. It was a sunny autumn afternoon, and I was the only patient indoors; through three sets of french windows in the opposite wall I could see most of the others, dressed in the bright blue suits and scarlet ties of the walking wounded, as they hobbled about the parkland surrounding the house. Their injuries had all been sustained not in battle but on the football field or (as in my case) in the gym.

I had arrived ten days before in an ambulance. My papers had somehow got lost on the way, but I was able to explain to Sister that I had been sent there to recuperate from a broken ankle after treatment in the orthopaedic ward of a hospital in Norwich. They had since turned up, but nothing in them explained the fact that, although the ankle was satisfactorily healing within its plaster cast, I was still so weak in myself that I could barely manage to make my own bed without collapsing. When I remarked on this, Sister muttered something about 'shock' in an unconvinced voice, and urged me to put my trust in occupational therapy.

The main buildings of the house were still inhabited by its owner, a widow to whom Sister referred as 'Lady Connie' and whose surname I had never happened to hear. The convalescent home was Lady Connie's war work. She had created a rank for herself ('Honorary Commandant') and had designed a personal uniform to wear when she considered herself on duty. This consisted of a navy blue skirt and tunic (the latter embellished by gold braid epaulettes), black stockings, stout brogues, a short red cape and a funny little hat pulled down over her ears with a low peaked brim. The uniform, especially the hat, gave a rather fierce aspect to Lady Connie's appearance, but this was misleading: she was extremely shy. For most of the time she remained concealed from us in her private quarters, but occasionally she would feel that she ought to make some sort of social contact with the invalid soldiers in her care. Announced in advance by Sister, she would come marching into her former ballroom and pause for a moment beside each of our beds – suggesting a cross between some rabid NCO conducting kit-inspection and the Princess Royal politely reviewing a troop of Girl Guides. But Lady Connie would be so paralysed by embarrassment that the whole ceremony would unfold in a sad, self-conscious silence.

The food in the convalescent home was very bad; I had lost my appetite so did not suffer from this as much as the other residents, who constantly but unavailingly complained. At breakfast the porridge was grey and glutinous and the black beetles imbedded in it as conspicuous and plentiful as the slugs in our lunchtime vegetables. One evening, an ENSA concert party invaded the ward and awkwardly entertained us while we sat on our beds – two ladies in Pierrette costumes, one a soprano specializing in Ivor Novello, Victor Herbert, Rudolph Friml and Sigmund Romberg, the other a *diseuse* whose digressive monologue was entitled 'Just Nattering'. We were an inattentive audience. Unknown to the performers, a scandalous event had taken place during the supper preceding the show. The main course, intended as a special treat, had been steak and kidney pie. When it was opened, something was revealed inside it that was clearly neither meat nor pastry. This object was difficult to identify by its size, shape, colour or consistency, and nobody volunteered to test it by taste. Could it perhaps be some monstrous mushroom? Amid some excitement, it was eventually recognized as a dirty dressing, which had presumably been removed from a patient's wound earlier in the day or week and mysteriously diverted from its proper destination down the incinerator to end up instead in the cooking pot.

When the concert party had left, our indignation about the dirty dressing in the steak and kidney pie erupted in open rebellion. We refused to turn in for the night until we had lodged an official protest. Sister (herself a little shaken by the incident) at last agreed to convey the substance of our grievance to Lady Connie, 'first thing in the morning'. She later reported back that Lady Connie had been appalled by the episode, and had sworn to make up for it in some way by providing us with an extra luxury. Reparation was made at the following evening meal, and took the form of a classic mayonnaise, scrupulously prepared from the finest ingredients by Lady Connie's own hands, as a substitute for the customary bottle of Heinz's Salad Cream.

Now, Sister's eye was suddenly caught by the squat figure of Lady Connie in her Commandant's uniform stumping past the french windows outside. 'I'd better see what she wants,' Sister said, and hurriedly left the room, tossing the two letters on to my bed.

One was from Denis. '... Kay sends lots of love,' he wrote. 'The doctor says she's making good progress and he may let her go home before Christmas. But if she does she'll have to take very great care of herself and won't be able to work or anything. She's worried about how her parents will react to this – thinks they would prefer her to stay where she is, but would also love to get out of paying the sanatorium fees if they can do so without it looking too bad. I must say, they do sound a nightmare couple. I shall miss Kay if she does leave (it looks as if I'm stuck here for another year at least). She's so wonderfully restful. She'll creep into my room while I'm sketching or reading or just day-dreaming and she'll sit there for hours knitting something she's making for Sandy – she *says* it's meant to be a Balaclava Helmet but it looks to me suspiciously like a Pixie Hood! – and even when we hardly exchange two words she's somehow very consoling company. Or I go to *her* room and try to make her laugh while she's washing her hair. The other day I did it up for her in a Victory Roll but it collapsed after five minutes. Only there is something tragic about her, isn't there? I've never known anybody with so little confidence. I suppose the trouble is that she's madly in love with Sandy. From what she says he sounds very glamorous. Do write and tell me what he's like – I long to know. Bet you dollars to doughnuts he's really queer as a coot (you can't fool Mother, dear!), but when I

72

said so to Kay she got rather heated and swore it wasn't true. My guess is he's the pseudo-hearty kind who pretend to be normal and stalk about the place being terribly, terribly manly. *Mee-ow*! I sound just like Ros Russell in *The Women*, don't I? I can't think why I said that about Sandy – it just popped out! I've always sworn I would never turn into one of those dreary old queens who try to make out that everybody else is queer too – no, dear, that sort of behaviour is definitely *not* my *tasse de thé* – so I take it all back!'

The other letter was from my mother. '... Darling, I do think it's worrying that you go on having such a high temperature when you've only broken your ankle! Do please get the doctor there – if there is one – to examine you properly. If only I was well enough I'd come up myself. The woman who owns the house you're in turns out to be an old friend of Dodo's. Apparently she used to be called Connie Phipps and Dodo says she's "a sweetie". Listen, darling, *please* make yourself known to her and mention Dodo's name and draw her attention to the fact that you *shouldn't* be having this fever when all you've done is hurt your foot and ask her to get a second medical opinion!'

Reading the letters had brought on a fit of dizziness, and I lay back on my pillow to rest. Could Lady Connie possibly be the racing aunt whose social judgments had been so frequently quoted by her namesake Billy Phipps? Before I dozed off, I decided that – even if it should turn out that my friendship with her nephew and hers with Dodo did in fact establish a double link between Lady Connie and myself – her own shyness, to say nothing of mine, made it quite out of the question for me ever to 'make myself known' to her ...

I had been called up about three months earlier, in the summer of 1943, as a private in the Infantry. After a few weeks of preliminary training near London, the batch of recruits in which I found myself had been moved to

Norwich for a slightly more intensive course. My companions in the draft were either youths of my own age (just nineteen) or mature men twenty years older, and there was considerable rivalry, amounting on occasion to hostility, between the two groups. Although still under forty, the seniors seemed to the rest of us revoltingly decrepit, with their false teeth, thinning hair and pot bellies; while we were resented by them as spoilt, insolent youngsters for whom the discomforts of communal life must be comparatively easy to bear, who should therefore volunteer to relieve our elders and betters of some of their more arduous duties, and whose failure to do so showed a deplorable lack of respect.

Two of my fellow-conscripts had worked in civilian life as apprentice cinema projectionists; their professional expertise happily coincided with my amateur obsession and I was able to talk about film stars with them in the same compulsive detail as I might have done with Denis or Kay. On free evenings the three of us would spruce ourselves up and descend the hill from Britannia Barracks to the town centre. After a cup of tea and a slice of cake at a NAAFI or Church Army canteen, we would sit together through a double feature. Once I deserted the others and paid a solitary visit to the live theatre: but the entertainment on offer happened to be a CEMA tour of the Ballets Jooss in a renowned piece of expressionist mime called 'The Green Table, and I was punished for my pretentious defection by extreme boredom. On other occasions when I felt a need to be alone I would go off by myself and sit in the railway station. This was one of the most depressing spots in the city, but when one is confined by circumstances in a place where one has no wish to be the nearest station can seem an exotic symbol of release or escape. In the gloom of the dirty waiting-room and the squalor of the dingy buffet I could imagine myself a little nearer to the metropolitan glamour of London and, beyond that, the security of home.

After the course of training at Britannia Barracks was over, I was due to appear before a Selection Board with the idea of trying for a commission – but I had made up my mind that, nearer the time, I would somehow get out of going. I disliked everything about the life of a private soldier except for the total lack of responsibility that went with it and which helped one to endure the rest by allowing one to live almost entirely in the present – an advantage denied, of course, to officers and NCOs. There was nothing pleasant about the grumbling, obedient, boring existence I was leading, but it seemed to me that the removal of all options except the most limited and immediate had also to some extent removed the element of anxiety. With nothing to look forward to, one might at least have the negative consolation of also having nothing to dread. When I found that I was dreading the Selection Board, it struck me that I should exercise the last option I was likely to be offered by choosing to remain in the ranks.

But of course there is always *something* left to dread, and for us at Britannia Barracks it was a forced march lasting two days which was scheduled to take place shortly before the end of our training period. This climactic test was persistently evoked by our NCOs as an ultimate terror with which to cow us into submission or exhort us to greater effort. The daytime ordeal (during which we were to be heavily clothed and weighed down with rifle, pack and gas mask) would be much tougher physical exercise than any we had so far undertaken, but this in itself was apparently nothing to the psychological torment of the night in between, spent on the floor of a rat-infested barn in some distant farm. 'The rats run over your face while you're trying to sleep!' we repeated to each other with the pleasurable excitement – and also the genuine fear – of children discussing a forbidden horror movie. In the event, the dread turned out to have been unnecessary – at least as far as I was concerned. I was so tired when we reached the barn that I fell asleep at once and remained unconscious until woken in the morning. I never knew whether or not rats ran over my face and would not have cared if they had.

There was also something left for me to look forward to. I had successfully applied for a weekend's leave on compassionate grounds to visit my mother in a London nursing home where she was recovering from a hysterectomy. In order to turn the event into an extra special treat, she had booked me a room for one night at the Savoy Hotel. A comfortable bed with sheets and pillows, a private bath, breakfast brought to one's room: such luxuries had become almost past imagining ... On the Saturday after the march, I took a train to Liverpool Street Station. Arriving at midday, I bought the latest Agatha Christie from the bookstall, planning to read it in bed that night and add a perfect touch to the anticipated hedonistic paradise. I sat with my mother till evening; the operation had left her frighteningly weak and in uncharacteristically low spirits. When I checked into the Savoy, I was in a daze of worry and fatigue – too exhausted to enjoy the ritual bath, to take in the softness of the bed or to read more than a page of *The Moving Finger* before passing out in a heavy slumber from which I emerged ten hours later even further depleted of energy. The longed-for night of sensual ease and extravagant self-indulgence had proved in fact to be indistinguishable from the notoriously squalid endurance test of the doss-down in the barn.

I spent Sunday at the nursing home and then had to bear one of those long, tedious, desolate wartime journeys on the crowded train back to Norwich. Tightly packed against other travellers in the dim corridor, swaying in rhythm with them when the train was moving, rudely jolted and then dejectedly drooping with them when it suddenly stopped for no reason between stations and stayed stubbornly still for hours, I felt delirious with discomfort. As I finally plodded up the hill that led back to the Barracks, I knew for sure that I was ill. The next morning I reported sick, but the medical officer suspected me of 'swinging the lead' and refused to examine me. This comedy was repeated every morning for three more days.

The end of the course was approaching, and I had still said nothing about my reluctance to go before the War Office Selection Board. Then, during PT, I was confronted once more by a challenge which I had never found easy: to climb a vertical rope about twice my own height, to crawl upside down like a monkey the length of a second rope hung horizontally across the gym, and eventually to slide down a third rope on the other side. I had got half-way along the horizontal rope when, as in many a nightmare, I was convinced that I was going to fall. Fear of this possibility had induced a panic which made the accident a certainty; at the same time, I longed for the fall as a terrified dreamer longs to wake. So I fell. I was taken to hospital where my fractured ankle was set and my lower leg put in plaster of Paris, and a few days later I was forwarded like a parcel to Lady Connie's convalescent home on the Norfolk Broads ...

Beyond the french windows of her ballroom I could see Lady Connie pacing the garden in conversation with Sister. After a while Sister returned to my bedside. She looked rather put out, I thought. She told me that I was to be transported later that day back to the hospital from which I had come. Lady Connie had received a letter from a friend of hers advising this course. 'All most hush-hush,' said Sister. 'I've never approved of people going behind other people's backs, but I don't suppose that any of it's *your* fault. I've phoned the hospital and there's a bed there ready for you – not in Orthopaedic, mind, where you were before. No, this time they're putting you in the General Ward. Going up in the world, aren't we? Never mind, they're just going to run a few tests on you, nothing to get in a flap about. And I notice that you *still* haven't finished that belt, you bad lad!'

The tests revealed a pleural effusion of tubercular origin, and a large quantity of fluid was drained from my chest. If the pleurisy had been diagnosed sooner it would have been a minor malady, but the delay had nearly killed me. One thing was clear: my army career was over. The merest suspicion of TB in those days was enough to guarantee an immediate discharge from His Majesty's Forces as it was thought to be highly infectious. I lingered on where I was for a time, and was then brutally transferred to the TB Ward of another military hospital. This was a gloomy Gothic building near St Albans which had been a lunatic asylum before the war. Once again, my papers had been mislaid in transit and so my stay there was much longer than necessary. It was a grim experience, which I later managed to blot out almost completely from my memory. But I can still see the rows of thin naked torsos punctured by needle marks and surgical scars and hear the harrowing noises made by a patient having a haemorrhage – a common occurrence, which usually happened at night and often proved fatal. I tried not to think too often about Denis and Kay.

The calf of my leg had shrivelled within its plaster and itched maddeningly: the cast should have been taken off by now but among the horrors of the TB ward this was too trivial a complaint to mention. At last my papers were found and I was officially 'invalided out'. I moved to a private nursing home in London where my foot was released from its shackle and I began to take in the wonderful fact that I was already back in Civvy Street.

The classic treatment for TB had been to send the sufferer to a sanatorium, preferably in Switzerland, but the war had of course put an end to travel outside Britain and a fashionable lung specialist had initiated a remedy by which he claimed the illness could be cured, or at least held in check, in the patient's own home. It was simply a question of plenty of rest, lots of milk and graduated exercise. For the first week one went every day for a very short walk, but the extent of the exercise was gradually lengthened week by week until by the end of a year one was tramping for miles over the countryside. One went to bed at ten in the evening and got up at ten in the morning. Extra milk was made available to be consumed throughout the day. This was the régime prescribed to me for an indefinite period.

So by Christmas of the same year as my call-up I was back home again in the village where my mother (who had saved my life by getting Dodo to write to Lady Connie about my condition) was slowly recuperating from her operation; where our house and the whole village were filled with the officers and men of an American parachute regiment stationed in the vicinity of the aerodrome on the top of Larch Hill; and where Kay too had recently returned under strict orders that she must lead the life of an invalid and be protected as carefully as possible from all unnecessary exertion and any kind of stress.

The following year of 1944 – so crucial to the course of the war, so eventful for the rest of the world – was therefore passed by me in an atmosphere of remedially arrested development, of unnatural stasis sweetly prolonged. The late rise; the morning walk; the early lunch at the British Restaurant established in the Church Hall a few paces from our house; the afternoon lie-down; the stroll to the Post Office to see if anything had come by the afternoon post (only the morning post was delivered since Tom, the postmistress's nephew and friend of Kay, had joined the navy); the evening walk; the early night: such an existence confirmed in me a taste for boredom and inaction which, like a drug habit formed in youth, I was never to succeed in conquering. And in this existence Kay (whose circumstances, in many ways so different, yet essentially continued to parallel mine) was my companion, my confederate, my spiritual cell mate.

VII

'Would you believe it?' said Kay one day. 'Mummy's got an American! Wonders will never cease ... Quite a feat, at her age. I take off my hat to her.'

'Do you mean Colonel What's-it?' I asked. I knew that Sybil had established some social connection with the Commanding Officer of the parachute regiment (she claimed that a cousin of hers had known his mother in Boston) and on this pretext had been trying to get him to come to tea at Watermead.

'No, this is a GI, a kid of about twenty. She behaves as if he was a proper boyfriend but I don't think he *can* be – except that with these Americans anything seems possible. She met him at the Red Cross canteen up on the hill – she goes there to help out sometimes, on a voluntary basis. This boy came up to her and said he had never seen such lovely grey hair on anyone – quite an original line to shoot, don't you think? She was tickled pink and he hasn't left her alone since, and vice versa. Apparently he works as an army cook. It sounds to me as if he must be a pansy but I may be quite wrong, perhaps they spend hours together making passionate love. In which case all I can say is good luck to her – more power to her elbow, to coin a phrase. Though it does have its funny side. If it was *me* who was going out with a GI she'd be saying, "Typical of Kay, she's always been man-mad, my dear – anything in trousers!"'

'Is Charlie jealous?'

'I'm pretty sure he hasn't taken it in yet. Anyway, the

whole thing has certainly sweetened the atmosphere at home as far as I'm concerned. Butter wouldn't melt in Mummy's mouth nowadays. She's all over Daddy (out of guilt, I suppose), which makes him a lot easier to get on with – and she's even quite civil to me. So thank God for the army cook!'

We were taking an evening walk along the downs to the north of the village and the sun was beginning to set. Kay was sensitive to natural beauty but her dread of sounding 'arty' usually inhibited her from voicing her feelings in this respect. Now she stopped moving and stood staring at the sky. I heard her say under her breath, 'Makes you understand what Turner and those people were driving at ...' Suddenly a wolf-like figure detached itself from some nearby farm buildings and ran towards us, then halted in a pose reminiscent of *The Monarch of the Glen*. It was an Alsatian dog. Kay gasped. 'What a handsome creature!' she exclaimed. The dog trotted up to us and cautiously licked Kay's extended hand – then became more effusively affectionate, leaping up excitedly to lick her face. He accompanied us for a mile or so farther, and when we had turned back and were passing the farm a second time he made it clear that he did not intend to be left behind there.

'I wonder if this is where he lives?' said Kay. There seemed to be nobody much about, but after a search we came upon a youth inspecting a broken tractor.

'Does this dog belong to you?'

'Oh no, 'e don't belong to me.'

'Who does he belong to, do you know?'

'I don't know. Nobody don't know.'

'Then what's he doing here?'

'My Dad's minding 'im for a spell.'

'What's his name?'

''Avoc. Everybody knows 'Avoc but nobody don't know where 'e come from.'

'Well, you'd better hold on to him for a bit while we walk away,' said Kay, 'because I think he wants to follow me home and though I'd love to take him back with me I'm afraid it's not possible just at the moment. But, look, would it be all right if I came back tomorrow morning and took him out for a real walk then?'

The boy nodded. For a long time as we continued on our way back to the village we could hear the dog whining sadly as he struggled to shake off the boy's restraining grasp.

Kay kept her word and returned the next day: Havoc greeted her as if she had always belonged to him. After a week or so of worrying about his welfare and contriving to spend as much time with him as she could, it was plain that he had become the centre of Kay's life. There was no question of his being allowed to enter Watermead, but in spite of this handicap she managed to assume responsibility for his feeding, his exercise and his general care and was soon his acknowledged owner. As he had never known a permanent abode, he adapted easily to the rota of temporary lodgings which she organized for him – sometimes at the farm, sometimes with me, or with her friends at the garage and the paper shop and the Post Office, or with Mr and Mrs Tripp. We were part-time guardians who were only requested to watch over him at night: by day, he was inseparable from Kay.

He was not a pure-bred Alsatian and his appearance was somewhat battered – one of his ears looked as if another dog had taken a large bite out of it. But he was astonishingly beautiful. His colouring seemed to change as one looked at him: in some lights his markings appeared to be charcoal on cream, in others walnut on honey, and his coat contained further, fugitive, transitional tints – apricot, amber, mustard. It irritated Kay that he was already called Havoc: she thought it a silly name. How he had come by it was a mystery; it was in some ways so apt, and proved so difficult to supplant, that one might almost have fancied he had given it to himself. Kay announced that, whatever anyone believed, it was *not* his name, and that she had rechristened him Mustang. But nobody except for Kay (and sometimes, tentatively, myself) ever remembered to call him Mustang; when Kay referred to him thus, people did not understand what she was talking about, and neither did Havoc. Eventually she was forced to capitulate to the power of oral tradition and admit that 'Havoc' had stuck so firmly that it would be simpler if she authorized it as his rightful name and reverted to its use when addressing or discussing him.

Kay defied doctor's orders and resumed her part-time job at the NAAFI: the small salary helped to pay for Havoc's food and to settle the occasional vet's bill. Havoc would sit quietly in the canteen while she was on duty and the customers did not complain of his presence. 'I'm not telling the family that I'm back at the NAAFI,' Kay said.

'Might they object to your working so soon after being ill?' I asked.

'Good Heavens no, they wouldn't give a damn about that. What I'm afraid of is that if they knew I was earning again they'd expect me to contribute towards their household expenses.'

The pleasant atmosphere at Watermead brought about by Sybil's romance with the army cook soon soured, presumably because the affair had for some reason or another come to an end. Kay hoped that her own almost continual absence from the house would give her parents the minimum cause for complaint, but they had heard about her relationship with Havoc and resented the idea of the animal almost as much as they would have disliked his actual presence. 'Sybil and Charlie say that this dog is the last straw,' Dodo reported. 'But as they forbid it to come anywhere near the place, I don't really see what they're kicking up such a fuss about.'

Charlie imposed a curfew, insisting that Kay should get home every night in time for supper at eight o'clock, giving as his reason a paternal solicitude for her health. But her health could only suffer as a result, for if she was late by as little as three minutes she would find the front door locked implacably against her and she would have to walk through the damp meadows back to the village in search of a bed. Each evening, having fixed up Havoc's shelter for the night and exhausted by the demands of her intricate nomadic existence, Kay would have to make a nerve-racking decision: whether to hurry back to Watermead and risk just missing the deadline, or whether to defy Charlie's injunction altogether and stay until morning at whichever friend's house she happened to be. If she took the latter course, there would be a row; if she took the former course and miscalculated the time, there would be a row; if she took the former course and succeeded in gaining admittance to the Demarests' dining-room, there would not exactly be a row but the experience of sitting in silence through the ritual consumption of powdered egg omelette followed by either macaroni cheese or savoury rice – ignored, disapproved of and mysteriously disgraced – was in its way as painful.

Havoc was on the whole a biddable, friendly and good-tempered dog, but traumatic incidents in his buried past had left their mark on his character and he was capable of reacting to certain people and events in an unpredictable, neurotic way. He had been known to snap at strangers, perhaps even to bite them. I believe that his association with Kay, though it vastly improved the quality of his life, did some subtle harm to his reputation. Invariably seen hovering on the outskirts of the village in the company of this supposedly witch-like figure, Havoc began to be thought of in sinister terms by observers as (not quite literally) her demonic familiar. He became branded as a public danger; any unexplained deaths of chickens and other farm animals were automatically – and nearly always unfairly – blamed on him; householders felt themselves justified in throwing stones at him if he approached their property; farmers were heard to threaten that they would not hesitate to shoot him on sight. This

84

hint of impending persecution added an acute anxiety to the other difficulties confronting Kay in her already harassed life. When I was not in their company they often appeared to my imagination as hunted outcasts, Hagar and Ishmael abandoned and wandering in a psychic wilderness of their own creation; but when I went with them on our long − and ever longer − walks I regained my sense of proportion and recognized them as just my friend Kay (whose romantic nature and eccentric mannerisms were underpinned by conventional ethics and philistine tastes) out exercising her good-looking high-spirited dog.

Kay and I often talked about Denis on these walks. She was deeply attached to him, but this feeling was only expressed in a characteristically understated way. At the mention of his name her lips would twist in her reluctant, secret half-smile and she would say drily, 'I've a lot of time for Denis. He makes me laugh.' During the summer he wrote to us with the good news that after more than two years in the sanatorium he was at last on the point of leaving it and was looking for somewhere to stay in London. He sent me a birthday present − a King Penguin book called *Children as Artists* which was attracting attention at the time. The short, serious text was generously illustrated by paintings and drawings with such captions as '*Mummy*, by Shirley, age 4, pupil at an evacuated Nursery School'. On the flyleaf Denis had written, in the hectic, spiky capitals of an infant's script, with numerous erasures and ink blots: FROM BINKY STUART (EALING STUDIOS) TO AUNTIE AYMEE WIF LUVE. I thought this very funny although the full point of the joke went over my head and had to be explained to me later: launched in the 1930s as Britain's answer to Shirley Temple, Binkie Stuart had been a child star who failed to fulfil her early promise and was in fact so profoundly obscure that neither Kay nor I had ever heard of her.

Throughout that sleepy year of my TB cure at home (for even on our most strenuous walks I often felt as if I had not

85

fully woken and that the physical activity was only part of a dream) the conflict between Kay and her parents continued to provide me with an alternative object of interest and focus of concern to the real war raging in the outside world: the miniature is easier to contemplate than the immense. The almost nightly succession of rows and near-rows that took place at Watermead established a combustible but apparently static situation, like a magazine story endlessly strung out in serial instalments, which echoed aspects of the greater struggle. Of each, one knew that it could not go on for ever while helplessly suspecting that it might, defeat being too dreadful to imagine and peaceful victory too wonderful. In Kay's case, the crisis was reached on the very last day of 1944.

'I thought it would be tactful to spend New Year's Eve in the bosom of the family,' she explained, 'so I settled Havoc in for the night with Reg at the garage and got back to the house in time for supper. Well, there we were sitting as usual in dead silence having just finished the meal when imagine my horror on hearing his bark outside the dining-room window and then the sound of him scrabbling with his paws at the front door! I shall never understand what happened, he *knows* he's not supposed to set foot in Watermead and he's always been as good as gold about it. Reg swears that nothing occurred at the garage to upset him and says he can't think how Havoc gave him the slip. Anyway, there he was. Daddy had heard nothing, of course, and I thought the only thing to do was somehow to slip out of the house and try to persuade Havoc to go off on his own, or if the worst came to the worst take him back to the village myself. So I mumbled an apology, hoping they'd think I wanted to go to the lavatory, left the room and got out into the garden. Needless to say, Mummy hadn't missed a trick, and lost no time at all in putting Daddy in the picture.

'My dear, he went completely off his head. He rushed to the store-room where the fishing rods and Sandy's cricket things are kept and grabbed hold of an air-gun (which I had no idea was in the house) then tore upstairs to the first floor, flung open the window on the landing (breaking every black-out regulation, incidentally) and aiming it at Havoc he started to fire away as if he were in a butts shooting clay pigeons! He could easily have hit me by mistake but I was much too scared for Havoc to bother about that. As it happened, he missed us both. Havoc galloped off terrified into the darkness. I was too frightened to go back in the house so I followed him, worried sick that I'd never find him: but there he was, only two fields away, waiting for me quite quietly, as if everything was perfectly normal. So I took him back to the garage and then went on to the Tripps, who very sweetly let me spend the night on their sofa.'

It was now the morning of New Year's Day; Kay had arrived early at our house to tell us the news. 'One thing is certain – I've got to get Havoc out of here! I know it sounds absurd, but the truth often does – the fact is, this place has got too hot to hold us! I am quite literally convinced that if I don't rescue that dog his life will be in grave and imminent danger. So we're off to London – quite frankly, I'd rather face the V2 rockets than Daddy when he's in the kind of murderous mood that overcame him last night. He's got such a filthy temper that something like this is bound to happen again – and next time he might not miss.' Kay stood with hands on hips and head defiantly erect, like Joan Crawford as Julie in *Strange Cargo* about to be deported from one island penal colony to another. 'God knows how we'll get up to town or where we'll live when we do. But we'll manage somehow. I've been in tighter corners than this and something has always turned up.'

VIII

So Kay and Havoc left the village for ever in January 1945.
Mr Tripp drove them up to London in a small delivery van,
similar to the one that had brought me and the cake from
Oxford nearly three years before. Kay sat in the front seat
and Havoc crouched at the back, guarding the two small
suitcases that contained her entire possessions: his long
face could be seen frowning anxiously through the rear
window as the van moved off. Kay's last words to me had
been, 'I'll be all right – I can always go to Lady Le Neve's
for a bit.' A week or so later she wrote to me, giving me her
address, and soon after that I travelled up by train to visit
her.

Lady Le Neve was an old acquaintance of Kay's who had
been left a widow with a large house in Cadogan Square
where she continued to live alone, occasionally letting or
lending rooms to friends (and friends of friends) in an
amiably slapdash way. She opened the door to me herself –
an untidily dressed woman in late middle age with a vague
manner and a slight Irish brogue. The house was rambling,
dark and dusty, with stained glass windows and inglenooks
in unexpected and inconvenient places. She told me that
Kay was lodged on the top floor; when I was half-way up
the wide, shallow staircase (there was a capacious
Edwardian lift but it hadn't worked in an age) I was able to
locate her whereabouts more precisely by the sound of
Havoc's barks. As I drew nearer I could hear Kay's voice
gruffly reassuring him and as soon as she opened the door

he sprang forward to welcome me.

Although its position suggested that it had once formed part of the servants' quarters, the room gave an impression of space and comparative grandeur; perhaps it had originally been intended for use as a nursery. It was sparsely furnished with big solid pieces. Havoc's occupancy (indicated by basket, feeding bowls, etc.) was more evident than that of Kay, whose few clothes and accessories had been swallowed up in a heavy mahogany wardrobe. I noticed the usual film magazines on her bedside table with one battered library book – *Me* by Naomi Jacob, an old favourite – and on the mantelpiece an engraved invitation card from Doris, Lady Orr-Lewis, requesting the pleasure of Kay's company at a tea party *cum* committee meeting at which arrangements for a charity dance were to be discussed. The date of the tea party was already in the past. I guessed that this invitation had been sent at the suggestion of Lady Le Neve and that Kay had answered it in the negative, but that (as its survival on the mantelpiece implied) she found some faint cheer in contemplating its existence.

Kay was thinner than ever and looked tired but not unhappy. It struck me that, like a private in the ranks, she had become so preoccupied with the struggle to surmount each small, immediate obstacle in her journey through the day that she had no time left for conscious discontent. 'I'm terribly sorry but I'm going to have to rush you off the moment you've arrived,' she said, briskly clipping a lead on to Havoc's collar. 'I must fetch his food – if we leave it too late they'll have run out.' We set off on foot with Havoc to a shop near Victoria Station which sold horse meat. When we got there we found that a long, motionless queue had already formed outside it; we stood at the end of the line, feeling rather hopeless, but were soon illogically relieved to see that yet more people had joined it behind us. I gathered from Kay's conversation while we waited for the shop to open that Lady Le Neve was allowing her to stay at Cadogan Square rent free while she looked for a suit-able part-time job, and that even if Kay did find work she would charge her very little. 'Oh yes, she's a dear – and what's more she's nobody's fool, although she doesn't always let you know it. Thank God, she was brought up with animals in Ireland so she understands about Havoc and has no objection to his being in the house. The place may not be Buckingham Palace but it's perfectly civilized and it's what's known as a "good address" which of course means nothing but sounds well in interviews and things while I'm hunting around for gainful employ-ment.'

The horse meat eventually purchased, we went back to Lady Le Neve's and descended to a cavernous basement kitchen where Kay put it on to boil. A strong, sweet, unpleasant smell emerged from the saucepan and slowly rose to the top of the house, where it would still be discernible hours later. After Havoc had eaten, he curled up on Kay's bed to sleep and I took her to lunch at the Unity Restaurant in the King's Road. It seemed to me that she could hardly wait to finish her meal for fear of being late home and keeping Havoc from his walk. He was indeed awake and ready for us when we returned. We set off once more, this time for Hyde Park, where Kay produced Havoc's much-chewed stick from her shoulder-bag while he bounded and yelped with delight. The afternoon passed happily with the stick being thrown by Kay or myself and with Havoc tearing after it, ferociously worrying it for a time with bared snarling teeth and convulsive shakes of the head, only to trot peaceably back to us and lay it gently at our feet. As soon as he had done this, however, the fever of the chase was automatically rekindled, and he again flung himself about in wild sidelong prances, surrounding us in dizzy circles as he anticipated the excitement of yet another throw.

That evening, leaving Havoc shut up in Kay's room, we went to have a drink with Denis, who was living in a basement flat in Pimlico. 'It's all very *Fanny by Gaslight*,' he said as he admitted us, looking plumper, pinker and somehow more matronly than he had at Oxford. 'Come in, my dears – I want you to meet a friend of mine. This is Veronica Lake!' he announced impressively, indicating a weedy, anaemic youth in pale grey flannel trousers and an Aertex shirt.

Denis laughed at our looks of surprise. 'That's only her camp name on the Dilly – you should just see her when she's all got up in drag!'

'The Fabulous V – There'll Never Be Another,' said Veronica Lake self-consciously.

'The Fabulous One is maiding for me at the moment,' said Denis. 'You know, I've discovered something about myself since I came out of hospital. And what I've discovered is that I just *have* to be waited on. So there we are.'

'I know what you mean in a way,' said Kay. 'But I've always found it rather embarrassing having people fetching and carrying for me. It used to be such agony in the old days staying with friends in country houses when one was expected to tip the chambermaid and had no idea what to give her. There seemed to be no way of finding out without making an idiot of oneself. So one always ended up either leaving much too little, which made one seem frightfully stingy, or much too much, which made one look like a vulgar *nouveau riche*. And I simply *hated* being unpacked for – one was haunted by the fear that one's knickers were full of holes or something, and dreaded meeting the chambermaid's pitying gaze!'

'You wouldn't believe how pernickety Denis can be,' said Veronica Lake. 'Works me off me feet! Everything has to be just so – or else Madam throws a tantrum.'

Denis put on one of his funny voices and mouthed to us in an elaborately staged aside, 'Our Mavis is getting ever so independent these days!'

'Talk about bossy-boots,' Veronica Lake went on. 'It's

91

like being back in the Merchant Navy, picking up after that one!'

'Well – I like that!' said Denis in mock outrage. 'Just look who's talking! *She's* the bossy-boots, let me tell you! I call her Mrs Danvers. Stalking about the flat with a face of thunder and her *châtelaine* clanking against her private parts ... why, I hardly dare ask her permission to put on the kettle for a cup of tea. Talking of which, let's all have a drink ...' And, assuming his Hermione Gingold voice, Denis sang as he served us 'While you're working overtime – I'll be drinking gin and lime – I'd adore that – Would you like it too?'

'I've got lots of fascinating scandal to tell you,' he went on while we drank. 'I picked up a Yank the other day who worked in a big actors' agency in Hollywood before he was drafted, and he told me all the dirt about the sex life of the stars. I bet you'll never guess what Joan Crawford's favourite kink is. *Well*, my dear,' – Denis paused portentously – 'this person says that what she really likes best is peeing on people! An actor friend of his had an affair with her and was simply terrified when she suddenly stood up on the bed and loomed above him with her legs apart. When it dawned on him what she was going to do he said, "Wait just one moment, please," and dashed off to the bathroom to fetch one of those waterproof shower-caps!'

This story shocked and saddened Kay. She tried to smile at it but she could not control a slight flinching movement and the expression on her face was grave as she mumbled, 'Rather takes away from the glamour, what?' I had often thought that there was an unusual purity in her way of being a film fan and in her attitude towards the famous. She loved to read about them but had no desire to meet them and it offended her to hear ill of them. Her interest in their doings was respectful and protective, as free from hysterical hero-worship as it was from envy and spite. It was a sober hobby, absorbing but impersonal.

When the gin and lime juice had run out, Denis

suggested that we should all go on to a queer drinking club in Chelsea called the Rochester. As the four of us were crossing Sloane Square, an ugly tramp-like old man, who was selling papers on a corner, thrust his face into Denis's and, with a lewd grimace, shouted, ''Ullo, darlin', 'ow's yer bum off for spunk?' Kay and I were considerably taken aback by this insult, and even Veronica Lake clicked her tongue in disapproval like an affronted dowager, but Denis himself was obviously delighted. He gave the smelly old paper-seller a playful tap on the shoulder and drawled, with affectionate reproach, 'Bold number!' before continuing on his way with a beaming smile which seemed to embrace us, the tramp and every passer-by on the King's Road in a loose fraternity of complicit amusement.

The Rochester was designed to echo the pompously masculine atmosphere of more conventional clubs in and around St James's but it only succeeded in achieving a clumsy parody. Sporting prints, reproductions of Rowlandson and Gillray cartoons and caricatures by 'Spy' were hung too close together on fake Regency striped wallpaper; those members who were not in khaki wore cavalry twill trousers, fancy waistcoats and tweed hacking jackets with leather elbows and aggressive vents; there was a depressing smell of expensive hair oil, male sweat and sewage (it transpired that the lavatory cistern was out of order). Veronica Lake seemed somewhat awed by these pseudo-hearty surroundings; Denis clearly thought them a great joke.

'It doesn't *look* very promising,' he conceded, 'but what I always say is, you never can tell. I've got a funny feeling that this is going to be one of those wild nights when one meets the person who changes one's life for ever. One wouldn't *expect* to find him at the Rochester (I know what you're going to say, dear) but odder things have happened.'

'I don't want to be a spoilsport,' said Kay, 'but I'm worried that you're not taking nearly enough care of your health. Too many wild nights can't be good for you – and I'm not at all sure that living in a basement flat is a sensible idea for someone with your chest.'

'Oh, it's only for a short time,' said Denis. 'I've met a very kind and generous person who likes my painting and he says the same as you do. The wonderful thing is that he's awfully rich and as soon as the war is over – or even sooner, if it becomes possible – he's going to send me to one of those very grand and expensive sanatoriums in Switzerland for a proper cure. So until then I'm determined to burn the candle at both ends like Edna St Vincent Millay.' Denis then gave a piercing imitation of Joan Cross as Violetta singing 'Sempre Libera' from *La Traviata*.

Well before closing time, Kay began to worry that Havoc might be needing her; we left Denis and Veronica Lake in the Rochester and made our way, rather tipsily, back to her room. I had missed the last train and Kay invited me to sleep on her floor. After taking Havoc for one final run round Cadogan Square, we settled in for the night. Havoc spurned his basket and slept on Kay's bed with his body stretched across the lower end so that she was unable to move her legs. I wrapped myself in Havoc's rug and curled up comfortably on the carpet. The next morning, we all three walked through Hyde Park to Kensington Gardens where I said goodbye to them near the Peter Pan statue and went off on my own to Paddington Station. Kay called out cheerfully after me, 'Oh, and if you should chance to run into Mummy or Daddy, remember to give them my hate!'

As it happened, I *did* run into Sybil Demarest in the High Street quite soon after my return. It was a rainy day and she was wearing a voluminous oilskin coat and a heavy sou'wester. She was also carrying an umbrella which the wind had evidently blown inside out and from which naked spokes were dangerously protruding. 'If there is one thing I cannot abide', she said, 'it is shoddy workmanship. What is more, I refuse point-blank to put up with it. I bought this umbrella in good faith – and it wasn't cheap, I may say – but that is by the by. I have never objected to paying out good money for good service. But in this case I'm very sorry to say that I consider I have been cheated. The woman who sold me this umbrella is quite simply a criminal, neither more nor less. And I have no intention of letting it rest at that. All through my life, I have been governed by one golden rule – and I'm perfectly prepared to tell you or anyone else who happens to be interested what it is. *Always go to the top.* Don't waste time footling around with underlings or middlemen – there's no earthly point and life's too short. Find out who's boss and go *straight* to him – or to her, as the case may be. And that is what I plan to do in this affair. So very shortly somebody who shall be nameless is in for a nasty shock and will be looking round for another job.'

'I was in London the other day and spent a nice evening with Kay,' I heard myself saying. Sybil's ice-blue eyes surveyed me from within the frame of her sou'wester with no change of expression. She did not so much ignore my remark as behave as if I had not spoken at all but had farted instead – had been responsible for a series of sounds which decent society could only pretend had never been made. 'I wish you a very good morning,' she said, quite kindly, and smoothly continued on her measured, purposeful mission to the umbrella shop.

A day or two later, the name of Demarest hit the newspaper headlines. Sandy, after several abortive attempts and months of ingenious preparation, had with three other prisoners of war succeeded in escaping from a camp in Germany by digging a tunnel under the noses of the guards. They had walked for miles through enemy territory, in the greatest danger of discovery, before reaching the sanctuary of liberated Europe. They were national heroes and would probably soon be decorated. We heard from Dodo that on his return to England Sandy had paid a short visit to Watermead, where his parents

95

were in ecstasies of triumphant pride; he was then posted to an RAF station in the Midlands to assist in the training of new recruits.

My mother wrote a polite note of congratulation to Sybil and received a polite reply. I was able to congratulate Charlie in person when, during a walk by the river, I came across him crouched on the bank, gazing into the water with apparent disapproval. He spoke so animatedly about Sandy's adventures and achievements that I found myself warming towards him. Either misled by this feeling, or prompted by an imp of defiance, I once again blurted out the information that I had seen Kay recently and spent a pleasant time with her. Charlie looked very grumpy indeed. 'I'm extremely sorry,' he muttered, 'but to be perfectly frank with you I haven't the faintest idea what you're talking about.' This was a formula he often used when his deafness had prevented him from following a conversation, but in this case I think he had heard what I said.

The next news I had of Kay was in early spring when she rang me up one evening in great distress. 'Thank God you're in! I felt I just *had* to talk to somebody who would understand and Lady Le Neve very sweetly said I could use her phone. I'm going nearly mad with worry – I've lost Havoc! Nothing like this has ever happened before and I'm desperately anxious about him. I've done everything I can think of – I've got in touch with the Battersea Dogs' Home and the RSPCA, and I've told the police who promise they'll do everything possible to find him. Actually it was a bit embarrassing because the awful truth is that I quite forgot to take out a dog licence for him – or rather I kept on meaning to but just never got round to it – and I was scared stiff the police would ask to see it, or somehow know that I didn't have one, but the subject never came up, I can't tell you how relieved I was. I swear to God that if he does come back the very first thing I'll do is buy him a licence!'

'How did it happen?'

'We were in the Park as usual this morning, quite near Bayswater Road, when some bloody car in the street made a funny noise which startled him and he went racing off in a panic before I could stop him and vanished behind some trees in the distance and I haven't seen hide nor hair of him since. I searched the Park for hours and hours but could find no trace of him at all. I can't think why he should suddenly take it into his head to run away like this – it's so unlike him. He *is* a nervous dog in some ways, I admit, but he's not normally frightened of anything so long as he's with me. And where on earth is he hiding? I'm quite sure nobody's stolen him – he would never let a stranger get near enough. The whole thing's a mystery – and damnably upsetting into the bargain!'

'Would you like me to come up tomorrow and help you look for him?'

'Oh, what a lovely idea. I knew you'd understand why I'm in such a state. But quite honestly, I'm not sure it wouldn't be better if you stayed where you are for a bit. You know how uncanny these animals can be and I think it's quite probable that he'll find his way across country, trying to get back to the places he associates with me. So if he should by any chance turn up in the village it would be a great load off my mind to know that you were there to take care of him and that you'd get in touch with me at once. The thought of his coming face to face with Daddy is too ghastly to contemplate! I'll give you Lady Le Neve's number – she says you can ring her up about this at any time.'

I said that I would definitely telephone in the morning to find out how the hunt for Havoc was progressing, whether I myself had anything to report or not.

'Oh, would you? How wonderful. I'd better ring off now, in case the police or anybody else has been trying to get through while we've been talking. I'm going to sit up by the telephone all night praying that somebody will call to say they've found him — or better still that I'll suddenly hear his bark in the Square outside.'

The next morning I rang Lady Le Neve's number again and again but each time failed to get a reply. At last, early in the afternoon, the telephone was answered, rather breathlessly, by Lady Le Neve herself. She told me what had happened since I had spoken to Kay on the previous evening.

For a time, Kay had been true to her word and had patiently sat near the telephone waiting for it to ring. She was prepared for one of three possibilities: Havoc might appear at Cadogan Square, or he might instinctively undertake the long and difficult journey back to the neighbourhood of Watermead, or he might have been involved in some accident (run over by a car, shot by a frightened citizen or angry farmer, trapped in a strange building) in which case she could hope to be notified in due course by the police. But after a dismal, restless hour or so, while the telephone remained callously silent, a fourth alternative occurred to her: Havoc might return to the spot where he had left her. She was immediately convinced that this was the most likely development and, cursing herself for not having thought of it sooner, she frantically put on a coat and hurried back to Hyde Park, confidently expecting to find Havoc waiting for her at the place where he had last been seen. But there was no sign of him there.

Night fell, and Kay remained where she was: she felt more optimistic, less passively forlorn, in the open air with moonlight glinting on the barrage balloons than she had when settling in for her housebound lamplit vigil. She sat on a park bench and after a while she drifted into a trance-like half-sleep from which she was awakened, shivering, by the dawn. When she got back to Cadogan Square her teeth were chattering; she had clearly caught a chill which Lady Le Neve was afraid might turn into pneumonia. And she was spitting blood again.

'I got my own doctor to come round at once,' said Lady Le Neve, 'and he popped her straight into St George's Hospital where she's having the very best attention. I've just come from there – I took her round a few things she needed. So there's nothing for you to worry about – she'll be just fine now. I managed to reach her brother (he took a bit of finding) because I thought somebody in the family ought to know, and he's with her at this very moment, so she's as happy as a sandboy – bless her, poor soul.'

I thought I understood exactly how Kay had felt when she decided that some form of action (however apparently pointless) was preferable to an indefinite period of submissive waiting and, although she had instructed me to stay put in case Havoc should miraculously materialize at my front door, I determined to disobey her by travelling up to London as soon as I could in the hope of being some support to her there.

By the time I reached Paddington that evening, it was too late for Kay to receive visitors. I spent the night on a sofa in the sitting-room of Denis's flat. He was concerned about Kay, but had worries of his own. The Fabulous V had recently been arrested for soliciting in the Piccadilly Underground Gents and was out on bail awaiting trial. 'You can't imagine the drama – it's been a *cauchemar*!' said Denis. 'The irony is that she wasn't doing a thing, just having a perfectly innocent and rather pathetic pee. Luckily I got hold of this brilliant woman solicitor. She's a great big bulldike, dear, and she specializes in rescuing queens who get nicked in loos. The police are terrified of her. She comes tearing round and shouts at them and they let you off at once. Unfortunately the Fabulous One had completely lost her head and had already owned up to all kinds of dreadful and totally imaginary crimes before the solicitor arrived.'

'They got me in such a tizz that I didn't know what I was saying!' Veronica Lake complained. 'They've a way of putting words into one's mouth, if you know what I mean.

And then they locked me up in a tiny cell and left me there all night. If I rang the bell once I rang it a hundred times, but nobody paid the slightest attention. I think it's a disgrace, and I intend to say so when my case comes to court.'

'You'll do nothing of the kind, girl,' said Denis. 'What on earth did you expect? You were banged up in a police station, not staying in the Royal Suite at Claridge's!'

'I had to have some refreshment, didn't I?' said Veronica Lake indignantly.

I hurried to St George's Hospital as early as possible the following morning. After a long wait I was admitted to a crowded ward. I moved uncertainly from bed to bed until I recognized Kay. She was lying very still and she was smiling. Something about her – at the same time peaceful and intense – reminded me of her concentrated sunbathing sessions on the lawn at home.

'Sandy's been angelic,' she said. 'He's taking care of everything. I shan't have to stay in here for very long, the doctor says, but Sandy thinks that when I leave I ought to go back to Cornwall for a while and have a thorough rest, so he's making all the arrangements. Listen, I don't know *what* to do about Havoc. One thing I know for sure – if he's alive, he'll try to find me. I've asked Lady Le Neve to keep a look-out for him, but I still think he's more likely to make his way back to the village and if he does I think he'll try your place first. So when you see him, or if you have any other news of him, good or bad, will you promise to send me a telegram to the sanatorium at once?'

I promised. And when I got back to the village I waited for him. But he didn't come and I never saw him again.

IX

My twenty-first birthday was spent alone at home. It fell on a Sunday in the summer of 1945, half-way through that ambiguous period of fourteen weeks which separated VE Day from VJ Day – a trancelike hiatus of anticipated relief poised between war and peace. Those rooms in our house which for nearly six years had been occupied by British or American military personnel were now empty, and badly in need of repair: their silence seemed to impose itself on the atmosphere as a positive force. My mother had put the place up for sale and was now staying with a friend in London, trying to secure the lease of a small house in Knightsbridge which had been damaged by the blast of a nearby bomb and might therefore be obtainable at a low rent without a premium. Soon I would be leaving the village for good. I was fiddling about with the radio, hoping to find some jazz on the American Forces Network, when I saw a jeep drive up to the front door. Assuming that it belonged to a prospective buyer sent by the estate agent with an order to view, I hastened outside to admit the visitor. But the man who stepped down from the jeep was Sandy Demarest.

He was wearing the uniform of the RAF, in which he had reached the rank of Group-Captain. Sandy was only thirty-five but his wartime experience had aged him. His face was as handsome as ever but had become almost haggard, the lined skin stretched thinly over the gaunt bones. His fine dark eyes still burned, but their glance had grown remote. One felt that he had survived his various ordeals (suicidal missions, humiliating captivity, daredevil escapes) unmaimed though not unhurt. Perhaps heroism must of necessity desensitize in one way or another: in Sandy's case, a stylized manner originally assumed as protective armour had hardened yet further under adversity to a point where it paradoxically rendered him endearingly defenceless.

'I cannot begin to describe to you the depths of corruption to which I was forced to sink – the whopping lies I had to tell and the shameless bribes I had to offer – in order to get hold of this jeep!' he said, after I had ushered him indoors. 'I have no right to it at all, really – not nearly grand enough! But thank God I did. I've just been down to see our darling girl in Cornwall. Frankly, I couldn't have faced the journey by train. And as I had to pass by your gates on my way back to London I thought I'd just pop in on the off-chance of finding you at home. Kay particularly wanted me to see you and give you her love in person. As a matter of fact, she entrusted me with a special message for you, under strict instructions to deliver it without fail when next we met. So here goes. It doesn't seem to me to make any sense at all, but no doubt you'll understand what she's driving at. She said, "Ask him if he remembers the time when he came with the cake." I do hope it doesn't mean anything too rude!'

'How is she?'

'In great heart. Yes, in great heart. Of course, she's been having a very thin time of it for a while now, poor love ... One thing, they're allowing her to smoke again, so she's thoroughly enjoying that. You remember what a chimney she used to be? She nearly went mad when they told her she had to give it up.'

'But that must mean they think the TB's almost cured?'

'No, old boy, I'm afraid not. In fact, it means quite the opposite ... Look, I've got to get back on the road at once, but before I do could I borrow your telephone for just one local call? I might as well ring home now that I'm so near. Of course, they've no idea where I've been ...'

He spoke for some time on the telephone to both his mother and his father while I tried to avoid confronting the significance of what he had implied – that Kay's doctor no longer thought it was worth while forbidding her to smoke. When he had hung up, he explained, 'I didn't say where I was – better to let them think I was calling from London – it seemed easier that way. Once the old girl cottoned on to the fact that I'm in the neighbourhood she'd want to know what I was doing here and if I told her the truth about Cornwall – I mean, that I'd visited Kay on the sly – it would only upset her and then the fat would be well and truly in the fire. So should you run into either of them in the street, don't say anything about having seen me, there's a good man.'

'But surely they *couldn't* mind your wanting to be with Kay when she's been so terribly ill?'

I regretted my outburst when I saw the expression on Sandy's face. It was one of deep and dangerous exhaustion.

'There'd be a row, you see, and I just – could – not – stand it,' he said, smiling gently and spacing the words to give them an emphasis of quiet desperation. 'I've been through quite enough already over the past few days. Please forgive me, but I can't bear to talk about it. Darling Kay ... it was harrowing ... we neither of us said so, but we both knew it was goodbye ... Listen, *I* must say goodbye this very minute, I really must. I've got this important meeting tonight in London with a movie producer and it would never do to keep him waiting. I'm going to be demobbed at any moment and I've just got to find myself a job. This chap might have a part for me in his next film. It's one of those beastly war epics, something to do with the Battle of Britain ... so wish me luck!'

Although he was now talking almost jauntily, Sandy still looked stricken. When we parted he squeezed my shoulder hard and then gave it a little pat.

103

It was only after he had driven off that I took in fully what he had been trying to tell me. He was clearly convinced that very soon Kay was going to die. She was presumably too ill to see anyone outside her immediate family and therefore, as far as I was concerned, she might as well have been already dead. I began to realize that I would never see her again. Feeling trapped by grief, I instinctively left the house, as though it were possible to leave the grief behind there, but it only grew heavier the farther and faster I tried to walk away from it. I retraced my steps and sought refuge in the other garden, where I stood very still, bemusedly hoping that the grief might lessen if I made no move to attract its attention.

Little was left here of my father's orderly creation. The vegetable garden had been expanded to dominate most of the available space, and the small area that remained for ornamental plantation had become overgrown by weeds, beneath which traces of the original arrangement of ovals, crescents, triangles and circles could only faintly be perceived. The unclipped yews had long ago lost their animal shapes and the bird-baths, benches and sundial had been sold to an antique dealer in the High Street. The church bells were ringing as relentlessly as they had on VE Day, but on this occasion they were celebrating nothing more momentous than the imminence of Sunday Evening Service.

The bells made me think of the war that was nearly over and of the people who had died in it. It struck me as ironic that the same disease which was bringing Kay's life to a premature end in her fortieth year had very probably preserved mine. If I had not been invalided out of the army while I was still in training I would certainly have taken part in the Normandy landings of 1944 and might well have been killed then or later, as my friends at Britannia Barracks had been and so many others of my contemporaries – Billy Phipps and Harry Vokins among them.

Throughout the war I had somehow managed to keep

full awareness of its import on the edge of my consciousness, so that while I imagined I felt concern about the slaughter involved, I had not really been affected by it at a deep personal level. Why then was I touched so keenly by the approaching death of Kay? Was I so mean a spirit that I could only react to human tragedy if it occasioned a loss in my immediate circle? Or was it because I vaguely felt that if I had tried harder I might have done something to save her? Reviewing my relationship with Kay, I found no valid cause for remorse: if I had been guilty of sins of omission they had only been of a normally venial kind. Yet it was inescapably true that the sense of bereavement which now overwhelmed me with such frightening force was accompanied by an equally crushing sense of defeat, with its attendant emotions of anger and shame.

Seeking some comfort in righteous indignation by externalizing the responsibility and exaggerating the blame, I tried to see Kay's story in over-simplified terms of melodrama. She had to all intents and purposes been destroyed by her parents, and Sandy had morally colluded in the metaphorical murder, unmanned by the mysterious terror which that silly old bore Sybil Demarest seemed able to inspire in her family ... But I had to acknowledge that according to this interpretation my complicity in the alleged crime was at least as great as his, because in his absence I had witnessed every stage of its development and had still been incapable of preventing it.

I preferred to believe that nothing and nobody *could* have prevented it, that Kay was an inevitable casualty of one of those mock battles of which the outcome is predictable from the start because the winners have the ruthless will to victory and the losers are stubbornly committed to failure. For a moment she appeared to me as a martyr whose wasted life could be taken to symbolize an unholy triumph of corrupt compromise over artless purity. Then I seemed to hear Kay's cosy, laconic voice and to see her high-shouldered figure moving with the deliberate, deceptively confident steps of her 'tarty' walk, and I rejected as sentimental and patronizing the notion that she was a natural victim, fated from birth to frustration and despair. All the same, as a tribute to her memory, I romantically swore a loyal oath in the other garden that until my own death I would eschew ambition for worldly success and avoid the wielders of influence and power, choosing my friends among the innocently uncompetitive. It is not a vow that I have always been able to keep.